FTB

W.i.t.c.h.

Will   Irma   Taranee   Cornelia   Hay Lin

Path of Revenge

Adapted by **KATE EGAN**

an imprint of
HYPERION BOOKS FOR CHILDREN
New York

W.I.T.C.H. Will Irma Taranee Cornelia Hay Lin is a trademark of Disney Enterprises, Inc.
Volo® is a registered trademark of Disney Enterprises, Inc.
Volo/Hyperion Books for Children are imprints of Disney Children's Book Group, L.L.C.

Printed in the United States of America
First Edition
1 3 5 7 9 10 8 6 4 2

This book is set in 12/16.5 Hiroshige Book.
ISBN 0-7868-5277-1
Visit www.clubwitch.com

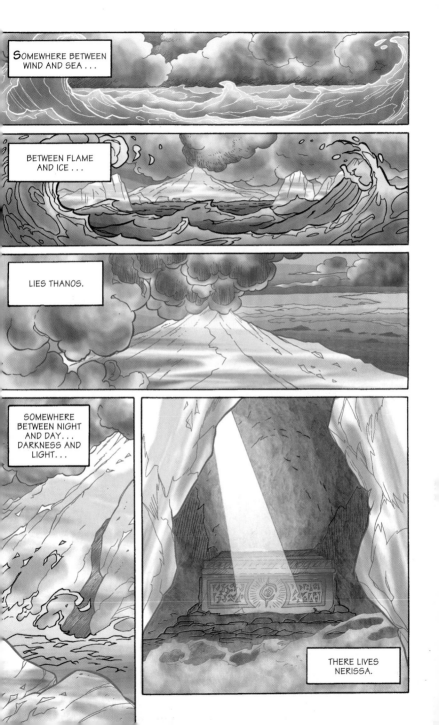

ONE

Irma Lair couldn't have been happier. Here she was, in her favorite vacation spot with all of her best friends! She was glad that Will, Taranee, Cornelia, and Hay Lin had all come with her to the beach for the week. Everyone had had different family vacation plans, but they had all been able to come to the Lairs' beach house for the first week of the school break.

While Irma thought Cormoran Beach was cool, she knew that the little cabin that the family had was a bit small. But after the last few weeks of bickering with her friends, she'd pretty much convinced herself that the cozy quarters would be a good way for the girls to have some quality time together.

Irma's family had rented a cabin in Camp Cormoran every summer for as long as she could remember. The cabins were wooden and rustic, nestled in a shady glade, and even Irma was into the back-to-nature thing when they were there. The best part of Camp Cormoran was that the beach was just steps away from the cabins. Cormoran Beach had everything a girl could want: comfy beach chairs, a snack bar, a volleyball net, and a different hunky life-guard every year. It was one of Irma's favorite places of all time.

Irma had always loved going to the beach with her family. But this year, things were going to be different: new and improved and better than ever. Forget about flying kites with Mom or building sand castles with Christopher, Irma had resolved. No kid stuff this year!

Irma went over the long list of things to do in her head.

Serious tanning, she thought. Floating on the waves and walking on the beach. Flirting with lifeguards. Ice cream by day and bonfires by night—and meeting lots of new kids. Plus, of course, catching up on what's new with my friends! It's been way too long since we were able to just chill out.

Irma hadn't seen that much of her friends lately. And when she had, they were dodging danger a lot more than hanging out. The five of them really needed a vacation.

It had all started way back at the beginning of the school year, when they were over at Hay Lin's apartment. The four friends hadn't known Will very well, because she was new in town. But strange things had been happening to all of them, and they'd been drawn to each other as if by magic.

That afternoon, Hay Lin's grandmother had told the girls their destiny. They had been chosen as the new Guardians of the Veil by a wise and benevolent being called the Oracle. He lived in a distant world called Candracar, suspended somewhere between time and infinity. The first time, they got there by crossing an air-colored bridge. But now they were able to journey to Candracar with the help of the Heart of Candracar.

A long time ago—like, centuries—the Oracle had created an invisible barrier, called the Veil, to protect the earth from another world, a world that had grown dark and dangerous: Metamoor. With the dawn of the new millennium, however, the Veil had started to become fragile. Now, portals, or openings, were appearing all over the Veil, making it easy to travel between the earth and Metamoor. If the portals weren't closed pretty soon, there was going to be trouble with the creatures coming through to the earth—which would be seriously bad news.

It just so happened that all of the portals were in the girls' hometown, Heatherfield. The Guardians were charged with closing the portals and making sure that the creatures from Metamoor couldn't get through. In order to complete this task, the girls were each given a special and unique power over one of several elements.

Irma's power was over water. Now she could do a lot more than bodysurf in the ocean. Irma could conjure up floods and create enormous waves.

Solid Cornelia had power over the earth, while easygoing Hay Lin controlled the air. Quiet Taranee surprised them all with her utter mastery over fire, and Will had the most amazing power of them all: she was the Keeper of the Heart of Candracar, a luminescent pink orb in a magnificent silver clasp that popped into the palm of her hand whenever she needed it.

The Heart drew the other four powers together, allowing the girls to do things none of them could manage alone. When Will summoned the Heart, each of the girls was transformed into a different version of herself—in an awesome outfit, to boot. Together, they could handle just about anything.

The Guardians came up with a name for their group—W.I.T.C.H., which took the first letter of each girl's name.

They closed the portals. They saved the world. It was that simple.

Then, thought Irma, Cornelia messed everything up. Well, not really, but it felt that way! The girl had an uncanny ability to attract boys. Maybe it was her long blond hair. Maybe it was the confident way she moved through the world, as if everyone and everything was bound to follow her. Whatever Cornelia had, boys—from this world and other worlds— swooned wherever she went. And Metamoor was no exception.

Metamoor's evil Prince Phobos had surrounded himself with creatures called Murmurers. These Murmurers were prisoners that Phobos had turned into flowers that now lived on his palace grounds. They became his spies, hearing all that went on in Metamoor and reporting it to the prince.

But one Murmurer, Caleb, was different. At first, Caleb was like the others, but when he developed a will of his own he stopped being a Murmurer and became a boy with strong convictions. He became the head of the rebel movement to overthrow Phobos. And he and Cornelia fell for each other the minute their eyes met. Well, actually, they had seen each other before . . . in dreams. Meeting each other was really a dream come true for them both.

Caleb helped the Guardians on some of their missions—and the Guardians helped him and his rebel troop defeat the dark prince.

But just when Prince Phobos was about to be ousted, he did something that none of them could have predicted. He turned Cornelia's Caleb, the victorious rebel leader, back into a helpless flower!

Cornelia was crushed. She brought her

boyfriend home and stayed constantly by his side, tending to him in his plant form.

Irma rolled her eyes just thinking about how inconsolable Cornelia had been when they had returned from Metamoor.

Pretty ridiculous, if you want my opinion, Irma thought. Cornelia was so busy showering attention on Caleb that she totally forgot about her friends—and W.I.T.C.H. Without Cornelia, W.I.T.C.H. pretty much fell apart.

Well, okay, maybe that wasn't the whole story, Irma had to admit. There was some other stuff, like our powers going haywire and all that. Still, if Cornelia had stuck with us, maybe none of it would have happened. As Will always said, we're always stronger when we are together.

Irma took a deep breath. Get a grip, she told herself firmly. It's over! Time for a little R & R. It's vacation time! Everything is back to normal. Caleb is back to his boy form and safely in Candracar. Metamoor is now a peaceful place with Queen Elyon, their friend, rightfully in power. And all five of us are here at the beach with no homework! As Irma's mother always said, it was time to put the past behind them.

Irma looked over at Cornelia.

We never saw eye to eye, Irma thought, even as little kids. Cornelia is a control freak—and let's just say I don't like to be controlled. But, hey, she's been through a rough time lately. Imagine transforming your boyfriend back into human form—only to find out he'll have to live in Candracar! That makes visits a little hard, and the place definitely doesn't get cell-phone service.

So what if she ditched us for a while? And so what if she's trying to hog the guest sofa? It's water under the bridge, the water girl giggled to herself. We're at Cormoran Beach. And I, Irma Lair, am about to have an awesome vacation with my friends!

"It's perfect!" Will said, looking around the cabin. "And if it means we can spend a whole week together, I'd even sleep on the floor."

Irma smiled to herself. "You'll get your wish, Will," she said. She hadn't told the girls yet, but sleeping bags were going to be needed. "We only have one pullout bed."

"And it's already taken!" Cornelia said, coming up behind Irma to peer into the guest room. "I'm allergic to sleeping bags!"

Irma turned to face Princess Cornelia. "What?"

"It's the truth," Cornelia said. She looked right at Irma with her arms crossed over her chest.

"I want to see a note from your doctor!" Irma spat back. She didn't want the high and mighty Cornelia to get away with a comment like that. Just because Cornelia was used to living in a luxury high-rise apartment didn't mean that she couldn't spend a week in a sleeping bag like the rest of them. A little slumming might even be good for her.

Before Irma could say anything, a pillow hit her squarely on the head. And then another came from the other side. Pillow fight!

"Um, well, see you next Saturday, girls!" Mr. Lair called, poking his head into the room. "Be good now, you hear?"

The pillows stopped flying, and Irma popped out of the pile. All five girls looked up at the sergeant, who was on his way back to finish an investigation in Heatherfield. "Okay, Mr. Lair! We promise!" they said all at once.

I wish he were staying, Irma thought. But as

long as he's not, I wish he would take pesky little Christopher!

Irma groaned to herself as she looked over at her annoying little brother. He was always such a pain.

Irma waved to her dad and watched him head outside toward his police van. He kissed Irma's mom good-bye. "Have fun, honey!" he said in a chipper voice.

Irma's mom sighed. "Take care, Tom!"

I'm sure she wishes that Dad were staying, too, Irma thought. It's not really a family vacation without him.

A feathery blow to Irma's face made her pick up a pillow and look around.

"Put that down!" Cornelia ordered as she glared at Taranee.

"So you want a part of the couch, do you?" Taranee teased. "Here!" She tossed two cushions at Cornelia's stomach. *Thump! Thump!* they went, as they hit their target.

"Get her!" Will cheered, throwing two more. *Thump! Thump!*

Irma hoisted a pillow over her head and aimed it at Cornelia. But Cornelia was too fast for her—she slipped through an open door and fled outside to the driveway, shrieking.

Cornelia's high-pitched screams couldn't compete with the sound of the police van's brakes.

Skreeeeek! Irma's dad skidded to a stop. His door flew open and his arm appeared, holding a small boy by the back of his collar. He'd found a stowaway in his van—and it was Irma's brother!

"But why?" Christopher wailed. "I don't want to stay here with all these girls!"

"Be brave, Christopher!" Sergeant Lair said in his law-enforcement voice. "You're the little man of the house now!" He lowered Irma's brother to the ground and drove away again, chuckling.

Busted! Irma gloated as she watched Christopher. She was never sorry to see him get in trouble.

Christopher put his hands on his hips and scowled. Irma's mom hugged him sympathetically. She looked down at Irma's pet turtle, which was still in his traveling bag. "It's going to be a lo-o-o-ong week, Leafy," she said.

Irma couldn't be mad at her mom. She couldn't even be mad at Christopher. She was in her favorite place with her favorite people—and there was no school for two weeks! Nothing could ruin this vacation, Irma thought, rejoicing. Not even her brother at his brattiest.

"Race you to the beach!" she called, tossing the pillow at her brother. It was still peak tanning time. Why waste another minute deciding who would sleep where?

Pretty soon Irma was in her favorite place—the ocean. The others followed. Irma stood knee deep in the water with seagulls soaring overhead. There were sailboats bobbing in the distance. It was the perfect day for the beginning of the perfect vacation.

We even look good, Irma thought as she looked at her friends around her. Everyone had brought a new suit for the occasion.

Irma had to smirk when she regarded Cornelia. Even when she was wearing a flowered blue bathing cap and goggles, she still looked good. Who'd she borrowed that bathing cap from? Irma wondered. Her mom? On anyone else, it would have been a fashion disaster.

Cornelia was shivering at the edge of the water.

"Come in, Cornelia!" Irma urged. The suit

will be hidden once you're underwater, she almost added.

"Come on in!" Taranee called. "The water's nice and warm! What are you afraid of?"

Cornelia looked a little timid. "It's you guys I'm afraid of," she said. "No pranks, okay?"

"Promise!" Will said, crossing her fingers so that Cornelia could see. "But come in! You can't learn to swim without getting wet!"

Cornelia shushed her. "Not so loud, Will, okay? Do you want everyone to know I can't even float?"

It was no surprise to the four friends that Cornelia couldn't swim, though it wasn't really public knowledge. Cornelia was an excellent ice-skater, but when the water wasn't frozen, Cornelia didn't want anything to do with it!

Water girl to the rescue! Irma thought grandly.

She marched up to Cornelia and pointed at herself with her thumb. "Not for long, kid!" she said. "Say hello to the best swimming coach in town!"

Cornelia squinted. "If that's the case, this must be a really small town." She always knew how to get to Irma.

Doesn't she see what I'm offering here? Irma wondered, throwing up her hands. Not just swimming lessons . . . but a temporary peace treaty!

"You're making fun of the wrong person, Corny!" Irma retorted. She loved to call Cornelia Corny—it never failed to get under her skin. "You know, I *could* accidentally let you sink!"

Cornelia lowered her goggles and got serious. "Okay," she said. "You got me. Where do we begin?"

"At the beginning," Irma said with a smile. "Now, just relax and lean forward. . . ." She supported Cornelia's body with her arms. "The water will hold you up! Don't stay all tense, and you'll see that you're floating!" Irma had never taught anyone to swim before, but it came to her naturally.

Cornelia squirmed and quivered. But eventually she did just as Irma suggested—for once.

"Hey, it's working," Cornelia said with surprise. Then she looked up at Irma. "You're not using your powers, are you?"

Irma shook her head but kept her arms still for Cornelia. "Nope, no magic! Now try flapping your arms and kicking your legs!"

Splash! Splash! Splash! Suddenly Irma was underwater. Was there a tidal wave? Was there an ocean liner cruising by? No, it was just Cornelia, windmilling her arms and legs—and kicking up more water than a passing whale!

Irma rubbed the salt water out of her eyes and pushed her sodden bangs away from her eyes. She took a deep breath. Irma reminded herself that the best teachers were always patient and generous. This wouldn't be a good time to laugh.

"How'd I do?" Cornelia asked, standing up in the shallow area to take a break.

Irma looked at her friend, who was trying so hard to learn a new skill. "Just great!" Irma chirped. She wrapped her arms around Cornelia again. "But let's try again. You ready?"

From out of the corner of her eye, Irma could see Will, Taranee, and Hay Lin heading into deeper water. They clambered onto a float and sat in the hot sun, chatting.

Eyeing Cornelia, Irma smiled. Just then, Cornelia didn't look like the Heatherfield Infielder that she was back at school. One thing was for sure: Cornelia was definitely more comfortable on solid ground than in the water. Even though the two girls were opposites—like water and earth—Cornelia was one of Irma's best friends. Thinking back on all that they and the others had been through that year, Irma knew that those girls were the best friends that she could ever hope to have. Their friendship was magic. And during this vacation, Irma was going to make sure they all got along . . . and that Cornelia learned how to swim!

TWO

Behind Irma, Cornelia stumbled up the hot sand to the prime spot that Will, Taranee, and Hay Lin had staked out. That spot looked as appealing to Cornelia as a mirage might look to a wanderer in the desert.

In a few more seconds, I will be sitting on solid ground, she thought through an exhausted haze. And then I can drink some water instead of soaking in it—and this time it won't be salt water!

Cornelia plopped into the beach chair closest to her friends and took off her bathing cap. She let her long blond hair fall down around her face. Then she draped a towel over her shoulders and lay back to drip dry.

Feeling the warm sun beat down on her

skin, Cornelia closed her eyes for a minute while her friends slathered sunscreen on one another's backs.

Learning to swim should be a cinch after what I've just been through with Caleb, she thought. What's a little humiliation compared to losing my true love? I found the strength to bring Caleb back to life. Then I found the courage to say good-bye! If I can do those things, well, I can do anything I set my mind to.

Cornelia had always been good at setting goals and pushing herself to reach them. But this time she was totally wiped out.

What's more tiring? she wondered. Trying to learn something new and different—or trying to keep my cool in front of my friends?

She resolved all of a sudden to forget about swimming.

Here's the real goal for this week, she thought: not to have a goal. To relax! To have fun! If I still know how.

She opened her eyes and looked around. The sky was sparkling and blue, and the ocean was crystal clear. Cornelia reached for her water bottle and took a long swig from it. She breathed in the fresh sea air, then turned to her friends. Cornelia felt as if she'd been away for a long time. What's new? she wanted to ask. But she felt as if she should already have known the answer. It still seemed a little strange to be with her friends instead of Caleb.

Will was lying next to her on a purple towel, soaking up the sun. Sure, she looked sophisticated in her camouflage-print two-piece. But the minute she moved, her image was ruined. That's when you could see the big yellow frog design beneath her, faded from the sun of many summers. Her towel had a big yellow frog on it—typical Will, Cornelia thought, laughing to herself.

Will stretched out her arms and sighed heavily. "I don't know about you," she said to her friends as they basked in the sun, "but I wish this moment would last forever. I haven't felt this good in a long time."

Cornelia smiled. Great minds think alike, she said to herself.

"I mean, it looks like everything is finally starting to work out," Will continued. "At home, everything's fine. School ended up going okay. . . ." Her voice trailed off as she smiled up at the sun.

Hay Lin lifted her sunglasses. Her eyes bored meaningfully into Will's. "And with Matt?" she asked.

"Right!" Cornelia cried, unable to stop herself from jumping up to sit on Will's towel. "What is up with Matt? We've been waiting *months* to find out what happened at the Lodelyday!"

"We finished your swimming lesson just in time, Cornelia!" Irma joked, nudging her. "Another minute in the water and we'd have missed the juicy details!"

Will pulled her frog towel tightly around her, but she couldn't hide the beet-red color of her face. "If I didn't tell you about it, it's because there's nothing to tell," she replied, looking intently at the sand like a person with something to hide.

"Do we believe her, girls?" Hay Lin asked her friends.

"Not for a second!" cried Taranee. "You'd better fess up, Will! We want to hear everything!"

Cornelia smiled at Will, who seemed really embarrassed by all the attention. She's never been one to tell about a date before, I guess,

Cornelia thought. That was my job. But not anymore. Someone else can definitely take a turn! She was through with dating for now, since she was in a *really* long-distance relationship.

Finally Will gave in. "Okay, okay," she said. "We had a date at the Lodelyday! It was a really swanky place. . . . You wouldn't believe it."

Cornelia knew that Lodelyday was one of the fanciest places in town, full of white linen and elegant china. She loved to get dressed up and go there whenever her family celebrated a special occasion. The Lodelyday was super-dressy . . . which meant that Matt must have worn a suit, Cornelia realized. She'd never seen him in anything but jeans and a T-shirt.

This story's getting good! she grinned to herself. Matt must really like Will if he went to so much trouble to impress her!

"I was so nervous!" Will said. "It was all so perfect! The decor . . . the music . . . the maître d' . . . It was like being in a movie!"

Will let out a deep sigh.

Cornelia knew exactly what she was talking about. She loved hearing the details about dates almost as much as she loved going on them. Or used to, anyway.

"When we got there, Matt said to me, 'Will, you look gorgeous!' and then I was so embarrassed." Will even blushed as she told the story. "I couldn't look at him," she said. "I could only look at the ground and say thank you."

Cornelia shared a smile with Taranee, Irma, and Hay Lin.

Will shrugged and continued with the story. "Well, anyway . . . I looked around, and I kept wondering what I was doing there," she said.

"Eating, silly! It's a restaurant!" Hay Lin offered helpfully.

"Ignore her and keep talking," Irma demanded. She was practically drooling.

Will blushed again. "Okay, well, as I was saying . . . From the moment we walked in, we didn't say a word to each other. I was so embarrassed that I stalled by staring at the menu. But that didn't help—half of it was in some strange language. . . ."

That would be French, Cornelia added silently.

". . . I pretended to read it," Will continued,

"but the whole time, I was thinking of what to say."

She's hopeless! Cornelia thought with a coy smile.

"Then Matt looked up from the menu and spoke to me . . ." Will said.

"And? Well? What did he say?" Irma urged.

Imitating Matt, Will whispered, *"Um, well, I think I forgot my wallet at home!"*

"So I told him, well, these things happen," Will added in her own voice. She looked at all of us surrounding her. "Poor guy! He was so embarrassed he . . ." Will's voice trailed off because all of a sudden nobody was paying attention.

Cornelia couldn't help starting to laugh. She laughed so hard eventually that tears were streaming down her face. "'These things happen'?" she screamed.

Irma and Taranee had collapsed into each other, cackling, and Hay Lin was holding her sides as if they would split.

Will frowned. "I should've kept my mouth shut! You guys don't deserve to know!"

Uh-oh, thought Cornelia. We embarrassed her. And I know how she feels—they've teased me a million times about Caleb.

Cornelia made herself stop laughing and put her head on Will's shoulder. She had to hear the rest. "No, no," she said. "Please! What happened next?"

Will gave Cornelia a grateful look. Tuning everybody else out, she zoned in on Cornelia. "Well, I invited him to dinner someplace else. We had to eat, didn't we? So I suggested The Golden Diner."

Cornelia had to give Will points for creative thinking. The Golden Diner had the best triple-decker burger—and it was very reasonably priced! It was also the girls' favorite meeting place.

Will went on. "So Matt said, 'I swear, I'll pay you back every cent. Tonight you were supposed to be my guest.' And I said, 'Oh, forget about it—you can take me out the next time, to the Lodelyday, of course!'"

Avoiding Irma's gaze, Will went on: "Then he said, 'I'm glad to know there'll *be* a next time. After a screwup like that, I figured you wouldn't want to go out with me anymore!'

"I didn't know what to say," Will confided in her friends. "I was so surprised he cared at all.

I just stammered something strange like 'Um, are you kidding?'"

"And then?" Cornelia urged. She hoped that that wasn't the end of the story.

"I finally got a few words out," Will admitted. "I said, 'I think you're really nice, Matt, and I'd like to keep seeing you!' I think he's noticed that I've been busy—there's so much I wish I could tell him. . . ."

Will drifted off into dreamland for a minute.

Cornelia recognized that look. Will was in love! Cornelia cleared her throat, trying to get Will to finish the story.

"Oh, sorry!" Will said, brought back out of her reverie. "So, then he said, 'It hasn't been so easy to see you before, but I hope things can go better from now on.' And I promised him things would be different. I said, 'Count on it! It's been a complicated time for me, but now things are working out.'"

The same could be said for me, Cornelia thought. Complicated, to say the least! But now things are working out for me, too, I think. I feel more like my old self—especially being able to hang out with my friends again.

Cornelia grinned at Will. She was glad that

Will had found someone she really liked. That was the best feeling in the world—especially when the boy liked you back! She looked out at the waves crashing on the sand.

It's low tide for me right now, she thought. Things with Caleb are totally on hold with him being so far away. But it's high tide for Will—and I'm going to try to make sure that her love doesn't get washed up!

THREE

Why did I have to go and open my big mouth? Will wondered. My date with Matt was all I ever dreamed of, no matter what the girls think. I still remember the look in Matt's eyes, and the whole night was just perfect—well, perfect for me, anyway. And now everyone is criticizing every detail . . . and so am I!

There was something about saying all the details out loud that changed the story. Now that she shared the experience, the night didn't just belong to her and Matt. Having started, it was hard to stop the conversation—and the questions! Will hated feeling as if her friends were second-guessing her. But she realized that she loved talking about her date!

Will remembered the way she'd leaned

over the table and stared at her crush with her chin in her hands. "You're a special friend, Matt; I want you to know that," she'd said.

Matt had leaned toward her, as close as he could get with the table between them, and Will knew that he felt the same way, even though he didn't say a word.

We totally understand each other! Will thought, rejoicing. It's like we were meant to be together. I've never felt like this about a boy before!

Taranee poked her in the arm, jolting her out of her dreamy memory. "And then?" she asked.

"What do you mean, 'And then'?" Will asked, looking directly at Taranee, daring her to ask.

Taranee backed down, but Irma immediately began firing questions at her. "So what did he do then? Did he ask you to be his girlfriend? Did he kiss you?"

"We ate our burgers, okay?" Will said. "We were really hungry!" She wished she could stop talking, but she had a feeling that wasn't going to happen.

Irma shook her head and threw her hands

up in the air. . . . "I can't believe it!" she replied.

"And then we talked all night," Will gushed. "It was so nice!"

"Sure! Just great!" Irma said sarcastically. "When you see him again in September, he won't even recognize you! You let him slip right through your fingers!"

Will was stunned. Was Irma right?

Did I ruin everything? she wondered. That's not how it felt to me. But I'm totally clueless about how these things work. What if I missed some big sign or something? She considered it for a minute. No, she decided, Matt and I had a great time. Irma doesn't know what she's talking about.

"That's not true!" Will cried. "During vacation we'll be keeping in touch! This break came at a good time to think things over."

She tried to be subtle as she reached into her backpack. Was her cell phone on? she thought in a panic. What if she had missed his call?

"Can someone please talk some sense into her?" Irma demanded, looking around the circle for some support. Then she turned back to face Will. "Think over what? How can you talk about a break if you've never even gone out?" she asked.

She had a point, Will conceded silently. But Matt seemed okay with it. . . . It wasn't as if he had put up a fight.

Irma put her hands on her hips. "While you're thinking things over, Will, Matt's going to meet another girl!"

Will blinked rapidly and bit her lip with all her might.

I will not cry, she vowed. I will *not* cry.

She wished her cell phone would ring, just to show Irma how wrong she was, but it stayed silent. No one called. So Will resorted to using one of her mom's best lines, which always drove her crazy.

"Well, we'll have to wait," Will said as she looked at Irma. "You and I just see things differently, that's all."

"Enough!" Cornelia announced, stepping in between the feuding friends. "Time for an ice cream break."

Will would have jumped up and hugged Cornelia if she hadn't been so determined to act casual. She wasn't hungry. She didn't need a break for any ice cream. They'd only just gotten there—but she already needed a break from her friends. A lot more than I need a break from Matt, she almost said out loud.

"I'll have some later, maybe," Will said. "I just want to lie out and get some sun." She knew she sounded lame, but she didn't even care.

Cornelia shrugged, and then she, Hay Lin, and Taranee put on their flip-flops and started to head for the snack bar.

Irma lagged behind for a moment. "Are you mad about what I said?" she asked Will. She almost sounded sorry—which wasn't like her at all.

Will was caught off guard.

Am I mad? I guess so. Maybe. I don't even know! she thought. "No, Irma, really . . ." she stammered.

"Are you sure?"

"Totally sure!" Will nodded. But the voice inside her head whispered, *for now.*

Irma turned and ran to catch up with the others. Will was alone on the beach at last. She checked her phone one more time, just to make sure that no new calls had come in. Then she put on her hat and lay back on her towel, basking in the sunlight. She was ready to forget about Matt and just relax. That's what she was there for, after all.

I'm *not* mad at Irma, she decided. She's probably right. I like Matt, but something's stopping me. . . . Obviously, I don't know how to handle a boyfriend. Irma made that pretty clear.

But maybe it wasn't that simple.

Will thought about how complicated it was to have a boyfriend. Always choosing who to hang out with—your boyfriend or your friends. Always worrying about leaving somebody out. Will didn't know what that felt like, and she wasn't sure she wanted to.

But it's totally normal to worry about this, Will told herself. It doesn't have to stop me from going out with Matt.

Suddenly, two faces popped into her mind: Cornelia's and Caleb's.

What if these aren't the usual jitters? Will wondered. What if *they're* why I'm scared? Look at what happened to them. Cornelia was separated from Caleb in spite of the way they felt about each other. I saw what happened to them. I don't want to suffer like she did—no way. If Cornelia had a hard time handling it, well, I'd totally fall apart.

Then there's our whole secret-identity thing to keep up, Will mused. The W.I.T.C.H. thing. We don't know what we're supposed to be doing right now, but at least we're together. We're ready, willing, and able. What if there's some mission ahead of us? What if I have to disappear somewhere? What am I gonna tell Matt? "Can't make the movie, I've got to go track down some bad guys who are trying to ruin our world as we know it"? It would never work. How can we be together if I have to hide a big part of myself? I'd have to keep avoiding things and telling little white lies. No way, I'm not up for that. I'm all about honesty in a relationship—even if I've never really had one.

Will felt discouraged. But she couldn't help thinking about the date again. Matt had been so funny at the Lodelyday. Still, that wasn't his kind of place. It wasn't *their* kind of place. Will shuddered.

Will adjusted her towel and put a bandanna over her eyes. I just need to think things over, I guess, she told herself. I don't have to do anything this week except have fun with my friends. But eventually I'll have to make a decision. I have to think it over. . . . I have to look at this situation very carefully.

Will's questions tumbled over and over in her mind until she slowly drifted off to sleep in the sun.

She dreamed she was in the pool back in Heatherfield, swimming laps. Or maybe she was in the ocean—it was hard to tell. She was falling through a body of water, hurtling toward the bottom. And then a voice bubbled up from beneath her.

What is it that worries you, Will?

In her dream, Will's eyes opened wide. Nobody was near her, as far as she could tell. She was totally alone.

The voice continued. *There is a great weight bearing down on you! Something that oppresses you . . . and I know what it is!*

Will was confused. What was the weight? Matt? Her friends? Her relationship with her mom? Or all of the above? And whose business was it, anyway?

The voice grew angry. *It's the Heart of Candracar!* it hissed. *It chose you, and it won't set you free!*

A shudder rippled through Will, as if she'd swum into subterranean water that had never been warmed by the sun. "Who . . . who are you?" she stammered in her dream. "Who's talking?"

My name is not important, The voice cooed. *I am merely an old friend who wants to help you. Give me your radiant Heart, Will!*

Not a chance! Will thought. That's not the kind of friend I need!

She tried to swim up toward the surface, but she was moving in slow motion, and a strong current was dragging her down. She couldn't seem to get away.

Give it to me, and set yourself free from the suffering! the voice bellowed.

Will tucked her knees into her chest and propelled herself upward. She didn't have much control, though—the churning water turned her upside down. Will found herself gazing into water so deep she couldn't see the bottom. She was usually at home in the water, but now she was feeling scared.

And then something appeared out of the darkness: a pair of long, gnarled hands, reaching for her legs.

Give it to me, Will! the same voice screeched angrily. The hands grabbed her wrists and yanked her down ferociously.

"No! Let go!" Will shouted. She hit and kicked the water, struggling to free herself from the steely grip of the hands. The dreadful creature was intent on robbing her of her power—if it didn't drown her first.

Suddenly Will heard another voice.

"Who are you yelling at, Will?"

Will recognized it. It was Taranee's! Will's eyes flew open. She sat bolt upright on her towel and found her friend curiously staring at her.

"Wow! I had the weirdest nightmare!" Will said. She shielded her eyes as she adjusted to the bright sunlight. "It was all so . . . so real!"

How long have I been asleep? Will wondered hazily. Taranee hasn't finished her ice-cream cone—so I guess it wasn't that long. But then why do I feel like I have a sunburn on my hand?

Will raised her hand to her eyes and looked at it closely. A strange shape was emerging there, etched in purple. That was no sunburn! Will thought. The shape was a circle nested in an arc and crossed through by a jagged line. It looked as though it had been stamped on her hand by a hot iron—and it felt that way, too.

Taranee followed Will's gaze. "What's that?" she asked, drawing back in alarm.

"I don't know, but, man, does it hurt!" cried Will.

I'm going to sound crazy when I say this out loud, she thought. But it's the only explanation. And my friends have got to know.

"In my dream, a hand grabbed me right here on the wrist!" she explained. "Look at the design! It looks just like the Heart of Candracar!" The circle was the pink orb, and the arc was the clasp. The jagged line was the chain from which it hung.

Will clutched her hand in pain and tried to tell Taranee what had happened. It was hard to get the words out, but Will managed to say, "I heard a voice begging me to give her the Heart. And when I refused, she tried to grab me!"

The more Will thought about it, the surer she was. It's not a dream, she thought. It's a message. Somebody wants the Heart—and I have to stop them!

Now Irma, Hay Lin, and Cornelia gathered

around her towel. "What is going on?" Hay Lin asked.

Will let out a huge sigh of relief.

Here's all the help I need, she thought with satisfaction. I don't even need to tell them the whole dream—they're with me all the way.

It had been a long time since Will had felt so sure of W.I.T.C.H.

"There's one way to find out what's going on!" Will announced.

Will didn't need to explain what she meant.

"Gotcha!" cried Irma, taking charge. She knew just what to do. "Follow me!" She led her friends to a beach cabana, adding, "And let's hope nobody sees us!"

"Well, there's no reason to sneak around," Hay Lin quipped as the door closed behind them. "After all, superheroes do get changed in phone booths!"

Taranee giggled. "We're pretty super, too, for putting up with this!"

Everyone is laughing and kidding with each other—just like old times, Will observed. Everyone is getting along!

She welcomed the change . . . but it was time for her to focus.

It wasn't very long ago that her friends had been fighting and that their powers had been diminished. Will had ached to hold the Heart again. Now Will's eyes flashed furiously. Nobody will take the Heart away from me again! Nobody!

Will closed her eyes and put her burnt hand in the air, with the palm facing up. She didn't feel the pain now—just the anticipation of her magic bursting forth.

"Do your thing, Heart of Candracar! Take us to the Oracle!" she whispered.

FOUR

Hay Lin bounced for joy as billowy magic whirled and danced all around her. We're here! she breathed excitedly. We're in Candracar again!

She couldn't resist unfurling her wings for just a second—yes, she had wings, now that she had been transformed into her magical self. Hay Lin looked down at the flippy purple skirt and the sapphire-colored top that made up her magical attire. It felt good to be in her Guardian form again. Her long black pigtails flew as she turned her head quickly to get a look around.

We made it, thought Hay Lin. Now, where is she?

Hay Lin wasn't looking for the mysterious creature that had tried to steal the Heart. She wasn't looking for any of her friends—Hay Lin felt pretty sure they'd managed all right on their magical journey to Candracar. She was looking for her grandmother!

For as long as Hay Lin could remember, her grandmother had lived with their family in the apartment above their Chinese restaurant. Hay Lin still missed her grandmother, and it made her happy to think about the good times they had had together there.

Grandma laughed at all my jokes, Hay Lin remembered. She admired all my artwork. And she gave some great advice, too! Since she'd gone, nobody had been able to replace her, and Hay Lin was pretty sure no one ever would.

It was her grandmother who had told Hay Lin and her friends the astounding news that they'd been anointed Guardians of the Veil. Yan Lin knew what the job was all about, because, once, she'd been a Guardian herself. Hay Lin had been sure that her grandmother would help them find the portals and repair the Veil. After all, she had always helped Hay Lin with everything else.

But then something terrible had happened. Without any warning, her grandmother had grown very ill and passed away. Hay Lin counted the months on her fingers sadly. *It hasn't even been that long,* she realized, *and I'm still not used to her not being around all the time. At all.*

If there's anything good about the situation I'm in now, Hay Lin thought, *it's that Grandma is right here, right now.*

Her grandmother had been transported to Candracar, where she had become the ethereal, immortal being she was now, advising the Oracle and observing what happened in the universe.

In theory, then, Hay Lin still got to see her grandmother. But in reality the Guardians were superbusy. They were never in Candracar for very long.

Maybe this time will be different, Hay Lin thought hopefully. *Maybe this time I'll really get to talk to her.*

When the swirling magic finally subsided, Hay Lin saw that she and her friends were standing near an intricately carved stone arch, deep inside the Temple of Candracar. Standing beside the arch, Hay Lin could see a tall stone tower stretching toward the clear blue sky like something out of a fairy tale.

I've never seen this place before, Hay Lin thought. Hey, it's a new neighborhood. I can't believe I'm starting to know my way around here. Candracar is like my home away from home!

Just then, a figure swept toward the girls, her robes swishing against the stone. A familiar face crinkled in a smile, and a familiar voice said, "Come right in, girls! And follow me! I know a place where we'll be more comfortable!"

Hay Lin's heart did a backflip. It was her grandmother! She bounded after her toward the stone tower, then followed her up a long flight of stairs.

Her grandmother led the five girls into a round room that was open and airy. High above the rest of the Temple, it looked out onto the gleaming space where the Oracle liked to meditate.

"Is this your room?" Hay Lin asked her grandmother. It was beautiful, but Hay Lin couldn't help wishing her grandmother still had a room back on earth.

"It looks a bit like mine," Irma said.

"Sure does," Cornelia said drily. "It's identical. Especially the posters on the wall."

"And the size!" Taranee added.

The girls stopped laughing when Hay Lin's grandmother said quietly, "Let me see that design, Will." Hay Lin could instantly tell that her grandmother was worried about something.

Will touched the back of her hand one more time and then extended her arm. "Here it is," she said. "Let's hope you can explain."

Hay Lin's grandmother raised Will's hand and squinted at the design. She looked at the girl's hand from a few different angles. And then a dark cloud seemed to pass over her face— Hay Lin was sure she'd never seen her look so worried.

"Oh, no," she murmured, her voice catching. "Then it's true!"

"What's wrong, Grandma?" Hay Lin asked, a little nervously.

"It's happened, then! The Oracle warned me, but until the very end I was hoping it wasn't true!" Yan Lin wailed, covering her eyes. Her head sank into her hand, and for a moment, there was complete silence in the room. Then she stood up straight, clenching her fists and narrowing her eyes. "The traitor has awakened! Nerissa has returned!" she exclaimed fiercely. "And this," she said, touching Will's hand, "is her mark!"

Will looked up at Yan Lin with a mixture of surprise and horror. Glancing first at Irma, then at Taranee and Cornelia, Hay Lin knew they were all thinking the same thing. Their eyes all said, *This could be serious*.

Hay Lin's grandmother placed her hand on Will's shoulder. "Tell me about your dream, Will," she said kindly when Will looked up. "Tell me what you saw. Every detail can help us understand."

Will didn't seem to know what to say. "I—I already explained everything!"

Wait, Hay Lin thought. Am I missing something here? How does Grandma know this person, and who is she, anyway? Let's start at the beginning. "Just a minute, Grandma! First tell us . . ."

". . . Who Nerissa is," Cornelia interrupted. "You can't just tell us half the story!"

Yan Lin took Will's hand in her own, massaging it. "Nerissa is an ancient evil that I believed was conquered forever!" she started.

"Yet it seems I was mistaken."

Are those tears in the corners of her eyes? Hay Lin wondered. I don't think I've ever seen Grandma cry!

"Once it was I who had to remove all traces of her evildoing," Yan Lin said. "But now, I'm afraid, the task will be up to you."

She let go of Will's hand, and Will shook it in the air as if she were waking it up. Then she looked at her hand. "Hey, the mark is gone!" she cried in relief. The burn-mark was missing from the back of her hand.

I knew Grandma could fix this, Hay Lin thought, breathing a sigh of relief. Some things will never change.

But Yan Lin raised a palm in the air, as if she could read her granddaughter's mind. "Hold on a minute!" she warned.

Looking more closely at her grandmother's hand, Hay Lin gasped. The burn-mark was now on her grandmother's palm, burning into her flesh!

"No, Will!" Yan Lin said cryptically. "Pain never disappears completely. It hides, it finds a new dwelling, yet it is always there, ready to do harm. This is a fact of life you will most likely discover on your next journey."

She glided over to a reflecting pool in the center of the room. Rolling up her sleeves, she dipped her hand into the water. *Kz-zzak!* The water sizzled. "At times it may be erased as well," she explained. "There is much for you to learn."

Grandma isn't making sense, Hay Lin thought. Do we have a new mission? To get rid of Nerissa? Of this sign?

Hay Lin was not sure.

Once again, though, her grandmother seemed to know what she was thinking. "Perhaps the moment has come for you to know more," she said slowly. "Follow me!"

Without another word, she leaped into her reflecting pool. All Hay Lin could see was her hand, gesturing for them to dive in after her!

"Down there?" said Irma skeptically. "If we'd known, we'd have worn our swimsuits," she joked.

Hay Lin plunged in before she could hear anything else. I'm sticking with my grandma, she decided. I've never known her to let me down, and I don't think she will this time.

She was submerged in water for just a

moment before she landed on a slab of stone in a gigantic domed room. When she looked up, she could see that the top of the dome was the reflecting pool in the tower room. Beneath the pool, crystal walls stretched down and wrapped a cavernous space, which shone with the bright light that bounced off the brilliant cut glass. The place was spectacular!

Then Hay Lin looked down at her feet. The carved slab she stood on was just one of many suspended in midair, leading like a staircase toward the base of the dome. All around the stairs floated enormous blue bubbles.

Hay Lin didn't feel scared, exactly. She was in awe of this new place. Then, one by one, her friends appeared, and she had a feeling they were all feeling the same thing.

"Wow!" breathed Will.

"Oh, my!" said Cornelia.

"Have no fear!" proclaimed Yan Lin. "You are welcome in my crypt of memories!"

Okay, now I'm really curious, Hay Lin thought. What's the deal with this place?

She had a feeling that they were on the verge of learning something big. But she wasn't sure how she felt about it.

Now, I like an adventure as much as the next girl, Hay Lin told herself. I'm up for anything.

But she couldn't help feeling a little wistful, too. This wasn't the kind of visit with her grandmother she had had in mind!

FIVE

"Each member of the Congregation has his or her own crypt," Yan Lin explained to Hay Lin and her friends. "An endless life is made of endless memories—far too many to be kept within a single mind."

She put one foot in front of the other mechanically as she descended the slab stairs into the crypt, the five girls close behind her. All the memories of Yan Lin's long life were stored there, heaped beneath the crystal dome. They were her most prized possessions.

They come in all shapes and sizes, all colors and textures—like life itself, I suppose, thought Yan Lin.

Her memories were precious and price-less—particularly those concerning her sweet little granddaughter Hay Lin.

Usually, Yan Lin's heart sang as she approached the place where she might visit her memories. Each one was in a golden vessel, and Yan Lin had only to remove a jeweled stopper for the memory to play itself out again, right there in front her, almost like the home movies that Hay Lin never tired of watching back in Heatherfield.

But now Yan Lin approached her crypt of memories with a different feeling, one altogether unfamiliar: dread.

The bright, shiny memories were the ones on top. But below those lay another group of memories, long neglected and deeply tarnished. These were the memories of events Yan Lin had tried through all of her years to forget—yet it was these memories that she would be forced to regard now. She was not looking forward to it.

As she trudged down the steps to the bottom of the crypt, her thoughts continued to race.

How can this be happening? Yan Lin asked herself again and again. It was supposed to be impossible. What will we do? And how in the world will this ordeal end?

That was the one question Yan Lin feared, and the one question to which she had the answer. Wherever Nerissa was involved, she realized, danger and violence would follow. So how would Yan Lin protect these girls, the new Guardians? How would she prepare them for what they might face? And how would she ever manage to look after Hay Lin?

Yan Lin felt anguished by these worries, weighed down and twisted up inside. But she must not let the girls see her fear. She would lay out the facts for them as best she could. The girls had shown themselves to be wiser than their years. Now she had to allow them to make their own decisions, difficult as she knew that would be.

Watching one of the large blue bubbles that hovered over her memories, protecting them, she sighed. The bubbles looked delicate and fragile, but in fact their magic was what fed the memories, keeping them alive. They were as strong as they were beautiful.

How shall I begin? Yan Lin agonized. She considered several possibilities, finally settling on what was surely the part of the story that was most important for the girls to hear. It pained her to begin.

"The memory of Nerissa is the most unpleasant of all the memories contained here in this crypt. She represents Candracar's darkest hour," Yan Lin said.

"So, who is this Nerissa, anyway?" Will asked.

Ah, well, soon you shall find out for yourself, Yan Lin thought. And trust me, you do not want to know.

"Nerissa was once my best friend," she answered simply and sadly. "One of the ancient Guardians—and the most powerful. She was once what you are today! The Keeper of the Heart!"

Will looked astonished.

But she was the only one paying full attention. The other Guardians were still showing their amazement at the blue bubbles floating in space above them. There was Irma, poking one with her finger, then flinging herself onto another to see if she could squash it.

They are so young! Yan Lin sighed. And will they be so innocent when their newest task is finished?

Forcing herself to speak instead of dwelling on her fears, Yan Lin continued. "A long time ago," she explained, "long before you were born, there were five chosen ones. Besides me, there were Nerissa, Kadma, Halinor, and Cassidy." Images of the faces of those long-ago Guardians popped into Yan Lin's mind as she mentioned them. After all the time that had passed and all the damage that had been done, the memory stung almost as keenly as Nerissa's mark upon her palm. These had been her friends, and she always missed them.

"Together we faced all kinds of danger," Yan Lin said. "We were a fine group . . . until Nerissa decided to use the Heart of Candracar for selfish reasons!"

She found it difficult to go on. It was terrible to put the tragedy into words. "Nerissa was consumed by the Heart's infinite power, and wanted it solely for herself! The others and I tried to stop her . . . and we succeeded; yet we paid a very high price. Cassidy, the youngest of the five of us, perished in the battle," Yan Lin said, swallowing her tears and raising an angry fist to the glittering dome. "Eliminated by Nerissa, annihilated, as though she had never existed. It was a terrible, terrible thing."

Cassidy. The very name made Yan Lin shiver. Losing her had been more painful than losing a sister.

She leaned forward to describe Nerissa's punishment. It was very important for the girls to understand this part of the dreadful story that would change their lives.

"The Congregation sentenced Nerissa to exile in the depths of Mount Thanos, a place where water, air, earth, and fire melded together as one." Yan Lin pointed at each of the girls as she mentioned the elements they controlled. "They sealed her up in a tomb of stone. She was to have all of eternity to think about her crime. . . ."

Taranee interrupted. "But now she's back? How can that be?"

Yan Lin could tell she was trying to figure it out. She closed her eyes and rubbed her hands together in an effort to keep her composure. It would not do to let these young Guardians see the wounds of the old. They needed the facts, not her feelings.

Finally, she got the words out in a soft whisper. "There was a limit to Nerissa's sentence.

The Guardian would be set free only in the unlikely event that the five powers were united!"

Do these young Guardians follow what I am saying? Yan Lin wondered. Can they see where this is going?

"We thought that that would be impossible," she continued. "Yet, unfortunately, the impossible has come to pass."

Yan Lin looked at each of the girls, searching for their reactions. Will still appeared to be in shock.

Perhaps she wonders if this is all her fault, Yan Lin thought. Soon she will know that she's at the mercy of powers far larger than her own. And she will not be Nerissa's only target.

Irma and Cornelia had stopped fidgeting, but Yan Lin wondered if they were still distracted by the grandeur of the crypt. They didn't seem to be digesting what she was saying. Taranee, on the other hand, looked pensive and thoughtful. Yan Lin knew she had an agile mind. Perhaps she was beginning to understand.

A look of fear had crossed Hay Lin's face, and Yan Lin longed to do something—anything—to make that fear disappear. It hurt her more than almost anything she could imagine.

Yan Lin took a deep breath. Understanding was not going to be easy for these young Guardians. Pure evil was never an easy thing to accept.

SIX

Taranee's hair was standing up on end. Well, it always did that when she was transformed. The funky hairstyle was part of her magical look, multiple braids jutting out from her head at different angles. She liked to think it sent off serious "Don't mess with me" vibes, which came in handy, since she had often felt more scared than scary in her first outings as a Guardian. If anything, though, her hair stood up stiffer and straighter now than it ever had before. Right now she had a really good reason for being a scaredy-cat. That was because Taranee had a feeling she knew what Yan Lin was about to say.

I've had my suspicions for a while, Taranee thought. But do I really want to be right? Who wants to be the one who's fig-ured out a bit of cosmically bad news?

In her mind, Taranee ran through the series of events that she'd pieced together over the last several months.

When we got back from Metamoor, she remembered, after Elyon took the throne, Cornelia was holed up in her apartment with Caleb, and the rest of us were trying to act nor-mal, going to school. Soon we were squabbling with each other all the time, as if the pressure of being Guardians had finally gotten to us or something. And then, slowly, our powers started to disappear. Taranee remembered it all as if it were yesterday.

That was when Will's mom announced that she wanted a transfer out of Heatherfield, Taranee reminded herself. Will and her mom had been fighting a lot, and Mrs. Vandom thought they could use a fresh start someplace else.

Or not! Taranee mused. The four of us were barely speaking at that point, but we knew we couldn't let Will's mom leave under any cir-cumstances.

So we sneaked into Will's mom's office—

well, really her boss's office, Taranee thought, correcting herself—at Simultech to get our hands on her transfer orders. None of us could work magic on our own, she thought, but somehow Will still managed to unite us four through the Heart. We blasted a safe out of a wall—along with Will's mom's papers, which were inside. There was no way she'd be transferred after that.

But something else happened that we hadn't counted on, Taranee recalled. Where the safe had once been, a blue energy blob was staring out at us! It shifted shapes, looking like each one of us for a moment, then leaped out the window and headed downtown. We didn't know *what* it was—and then we didn't know *where* it was, either.

Taranee chewed her lip as she continued to remember. The blob was a lot more important than they had realized. It wasn't something they'd created on their own, but the end result of something that had happened in Candracar. It turned out that the girls' powers had been dwindling because their friendship had been weakening. And in Candracar, their Aurameres had been spinning away from one another. The

Aurameres were brightly colored orbs, droplets of magical essence representing each girl's special power. They rotated through the air in a sparkling chamber of the Temple that was guarded by a member of Candracar's Council of Elders, a creature named Luba. She was half cat and half woman, and, most importantly, she had never cared for the Guardians.

That was where things had started to get unclear for Taranee. Luba hadn't tried to bring the Aurameres back together, she'd deduced.

Luba hadn't tried to restore our friendship or our magic, Taranee remembered. Nope. She hadn't bothered. And it was even worse than that: she deliberately made our Aurameres collide! She deliberately messed with our powers!

Just thinking about it made Taranee's blood run cold—which was saying a lot, since she was the fiery one of the powerful five.

Luba never believed in us, she thought, not from the start. She thought we were too young to be Guardians or something. She thought we were irresponsible—even after we'd saved the universe. She was waiting for us to make a mistake, and she pounced on us as soon as we started fighting.

Luba had used her own magic to bring four of the Aurameres—all but Cornelia's—perilously close together. And when Will had called upon the Heart in that office at Simultech, there'd been a mighty explosion up in Candracar. The Aurameres had fused together to create a monstrosity called an Altermere!

Luba was ready to claim that it was all our fault, Taranee seethed. But it wasn't!

In Heatherfield, the Altermere just looked like a big blue blob. But the creature was a lot more deadly than it looked, Taranee knew. Within its constantly changing shape, the energy blob contained power over three of the elements—plus the Heart of Candracar. It was bent on acquiring power over the earth as well, and so it had stalked Cornelia till its power was complete! That's why it escaped into the city. If only we'd known what it was going to do next! Taranee thought.

Taranee's eyes fell on Yan Lin, and she knew she had to speak up.

She wasn't sure what to say. But she knew that she had to say something. Yan Lin obviously didn't want to spell it out.

"I think I understand," Taranee blurted out.

Then she simply said, "The Altermere!" It was clear to Taranee now. In creating the Altermere, Luba had unintentionally created a way for all five powers to be brought back together—and for Nerissa's sentence to be terminated. Luba had made the impossible possible.

Yan Lin nodded vigorously. Her eyes shone brightly. "Exactly, Taranee!" she said. "That creature absorbed your powers. Cornelia brought them together inside of herself and then transferred them to Caleb!"

When the blob had found Cornelia, she'd absorbed it—with all of its power. And in the brief time that she had been the most powerful person in the universe, she'd done what any lovesick girl would do: she'd brought her boyfriend, who had been transformed into a flower, back to his boy form. By that time, Luba realized what she'd done. She even tried to stop Cornelia. But by then she was unstoppable, and all she could do was scowl as the two reunited.

As punishment, Cornelia had been forced to leave Caleb behind in Candracar, Taranee recalled. It was a pretty serious punishment for what had been, after all, a mistake. Cornelia hadn't known she was violating the age-old laws of Candracar by using all five great powers at once. But, Taranee thought, it was a small price to pay when you looked at what her magic had done. The combination of the five powers had revived Caleb—and also Nerissa!

Now Will shook her head. "So this is all our fault!" she said. "That's why Luba was so mad at us!"

Taranee totally disagreed. Sure, they'd been fighting—and it wasn't what Guardians were supposed to do, but Luba was the one who created the Altermere! Without her interference, Nerissa would still be locked away.

"Forget about Luba," Yan Lin advised, narrowing her eyes. "We have another problem now." Taranee stifled her urge to explain everything to Will. Yan Lin had an important point.

Standing up from the bubble that she had been sitting on, the old woman paced around the crypt. Next to the place where her memories were piled, there was a magnificent space for what looked almost like a library. Tall shelves stretched toward the top of the glittering dome, and several books lay open on an ancient wooden desk. Yan Lin had obviously been reading up on the situation. Taranee hoped she knew what they were supposed to do now.

"The ancient Guardian is free once again, and she will soon return to strike," Yan Lin said wisely.

Taranee opened her mouth to speak. Was that what Will's dream meant? she wanted to ask. That Nerissa was on her way?

But Yan Lin put up her hand, and Taranee stayed silent. She was afraid to interrupt Hay Lin's grandmother just then—she had never seen her look so intense. Or so thoroughly freaked out.

"Nerissa wants the Heart of Candracar, and Will's dream has confirmed all of my fears!" Yan Lin cried. "She seeks revenge! Stay on your guard, girls! The enemy you have before you is terrible and heartless."

Yan Lin sat down on a bubble. She looked totally exhausted, practically ready to collapse. Taranee could tell that this was hard on her.

"But, Grandma, this is terrible! We—we're not ready for this! Tell us more!" Hay Lin pleaded.

Will was already thinking about the group's

next move. "When will she attack us?" she asked.

"And to think we should be relaxing on vacation!" Irma wailed, with extra melodrama in her voice.

Yan Lin sank back deeper into her seat. "I'm afraid we'll find out only when it happens," she sighed. She closed her eyes and folded her hands in her lap.

The Guardians kept looking at Yan Lin expectantly, as if she might say something more if they wished it hard enough.

But for some reason Taranee understood also that Yan Lin had given them all she had. Now the girls were on their own.

SEVEN

Nerissa seethed. For centuries, she thought, I was lulled by the sounds of Mount Thanos: the churning sea surrounding this desolate peak and the howling winds around the cliffs. And the roaring lava high above my head, gurgling over my lonely tomb. A lesser woman might have been lulled to sleep. But I drew strength from the energy of nature.

She smirked. They expected, she thought, that I would waste away in this barren place, the outside as frozen as an ice cap, the inside boiling like an inferno. The fools in Candracar cursed me as they sealed my tomb for all eternity, inscribing it with my story, the cautionary tale. I was to be banished. I was to be punished!

Once, she cackled to herself, I sought to seize the elements, to make them do my will. Now I am one with them! The ebb and flow of the tides have marked my days and nights. The storms have mirrored my rage. The molten lava has erupted, like my desire for revenge! The elements have been my only comfort in this exile. My only company. And now they are my inspiration! Their force is infinite and unstoppable. So, too, shall I be!

Throwing her head back, Nerissa screamed ferociously at the sky and the stars above her, until her voice began to grow hoarse.

How long has it been since I saw the stars? she wondered angrily. I make this solemn promise now: my retribution will be like nothing these stars have ever seen!

Her eyes left the clear sky and traveled downward to the ruins of her tomb. It had been split by a sudden flash of lightning, cracked open like an egg.

And so begins my rebirth! Nerissa nodded, twisting her rotten teeth into a grin. Nerissa was never happy. But a smile was in order, because now, for once, she had hope for the future.

Nerissa knew that only one thing could

have split her tomb in two. Her sentence was to be ended if, and only if, the five great powers of the universe were reunited. Nerissa could not explain how this had come to be. But there was no question the powers had been reunited, releasing her at last and plunging the universe into chaos.

I have been reborn in darkness to bring yet more darkness to the world! she cackled.

Tapping her long fingers impatiently, Nerissa began to recall the past. The events that had transpired centuries ago seemed to Nerissa as if they had happened yesterday. She wished that she had had a reflecting pool like the ones she remembered from Candracar.

It would help me, she thought, to look into other worlds, to assess threats and spy on my enemies. If only I could see clearly now. I must know what I will face when I emerge to seek my vengeance!

Suddenly, Nerissa found a solution to her problem. She stared into the red-hot flames, which shot from the volcano like water from a fountain. Sure enough, when she focused her magical vision, Nerissa could make out five shapes in the fire.

Oh, she breathed. Yes. Now I can see them. The new Guardians!

Nerissa could barely make out their faces, but she saw all she needed to judge the strength of her adversaries. She doubled over with laughter after her first look at the five of them.

They are so young! she snickered. They are so weak! They are so scared already, and we have not even met. They have no idea of the misery that is about to rain down upon them.

Nerissa corrected herself. Well, no, she remembered, now one of them knows that I am waiting for her. The one who controls the Heart. Or thinks she does, at least. Nerissa's body shook as she dreamed of controlling the Heart herself. Her eyes glazed over, and her soul shrieked, *It's mine! The Heart is mine!*

Longing for the Heart with every fiber of her being, Nerissa had no regrets over what she had done in its name. She felt no remorse for her many victims. All she knew was that every moment she spent apart from the Heart was sheer agony. Now, with every passing second, she drew closer to possessing it again. The Guardians were all that stood in her way, and they hadn't made much of an impression.

Nerissa squinted into the flames again. One of the Guardians looked familiar to her—and it wasn't the one she had chased through her dreams. Rather, it was the littlest of the new Guardians, with long hair in pigtails and a look of anguish on her face. She looked like someone Nerissa knew.

Yan Lin! Nerissa thought. But it can't be! It's true, the Guardians are immortal. But that does not mean they stay young forever. Could that be Yan Lin's descendant? It didn't take Nerissa long to answer her own question. Oh, yes, Yan Lin would make sure that one of her own remained in the service of Candracar.

When she thought about Yan Lin, Nerissa felt a strange emotion. For a second she felt something other than her desire for the Heart. "So many memories," she murmured. But Nerissa would not go down that road. She had no time for such weakness. She would not allow sentiment to stop her from holding the Heart in her hands once again! She had once been friends with Yan Lin, it was true. But it was so long ago that Nerissa could not—and would not—remember.

Nerissa noticed a shape cowering at the edge of the volcano. It was a thin and miserable dog, shivering in spite of the scorching heat. Nerissa went to him and snaked an arm around him, pointing into the flames, showing him the girl who looked so much like the young Yan Lin.

"Do you see her?" she demanded. "You will strike her first!"

The dog whimpered nervously.

He was the only one around to help her, like it or not, so she would use him. This dog would become Nerissa's servant.

The dog paced around the burning edge of Mount Thanos as Nerissa outlined her scheme. "We will destroy the new Guardians one after the other," she bellowed, "leaving the Keeper of the Heart for last!" This was the end of her humiliation, Nerissa vowed. This was the beginning of her retribution. "Yet today is a new day!" she screeched. "I will soon return to being as strong and powerful as I once was, and I will take care of the Keeper personally; oh, mark my words!"

When she was locked away, Nerissa had been stripped of her magic. But that hadn't stopped her from developing potent new powers, derived from the winds and rain and fed by the hot flames that surrounded her. Nerissa stretched her arms toward the whining dog, and blinding magic shot out from her fingertips.

Kraaak!

The magic surrounded the dog like a spotlight.

He pawed furiously at the ground. He was trying to resist.

"You will be cruel and fierce! Cold and relentless!" Nerissa cried as her spell began working to transform the animal. "I will bring you a new life!"

The dog arched his back and growled as he was engulfed in the white-hot magic. The light flashed around him and grew into a glowing ball, brighter and hotter than the interior of Mount Thanos itself. Strong winds whipped around the dog until even Nerissa had to stand back. She was pleased to see that her magic was overwhelming.

"You will be the first of my four Knights of Revenge!" she yowled.

Then with one final explosion, the magic winds disappeared, revealing a new figure: in the place where the dog had stood was a massive man. He wore thick armor across his chest, emblazoned with Nerissa's symbol, and boots heavy enough to crush anyone in his path. His wrists were encircled by spiked wristbands, and his gigantic hands were clearly capable of making sure that he would leave no trace of Nerissa's power behind when he began to do her bidding. Where the dog had been, there was now a monster—waiting to do Nerissa's will.

Kraaakzzzk!

Nerissa's magic shot still more energy into the man.

"From now on and forever," she commanded, "you will be known as Khor the Destroyer!"

Khor clenched his fists and lumbered toward her, the ground shaking with his every step.

Raaarrrgh!

His furious roar bounced off Mount Thanos and reverberated far out across the ocean toward distant lands.

Nerissa was pleased. Now another stream of her magic was wrapping itself around Khor, cocooning him for the journey to the Guardians.

"Go, Khor, and wreak havoc," she howled. "In the name of Nerissa!"

EIGHT

Cornelia crossed her arms over her chest and rubbed her hands together, trying to get warm. She'd already put on the pink sweater she'd brought for cold-weather emergencies, but she was still freezing. It was all she could do to keep her teeth from chattering.

After their journey to Candracar, the girls had returned in time for dinner. Now they sat outside the Lairs' cabin, each lost in their own thoughts. The information that Hay Lin's grandmother had given them was confusing and a bit scary. What evil was lurking out there? Were they in danger? Nobody was talking, but they all had the same questions.

Cornelia looked up at the threatening sky. The clouds were so dark they made it feel like nighttime. This is no regular storm, Cornelia thought. It's got to be a sign of bad things to come. Weather wasn't her specialty, but she was willing to bet that the dark skies were a warning.

Looking over at Will, Cornelia wondered what she was thinking. As the leader of W.I.T.C.H., Will was probably thinking about their next move. But did she have a plan? Cornelia hoped so, but she wasn't sure it was possible.

Do any of us even have a clue about what to do? Cornelia wondered. Yan Lin couldn't even tell us herself.

Cornelia wondered what her friends were thinking about their visit to Candracar. Not that anyone had mentioned it. Were they as stressed out as she was?

She was surprised by a rumbling sound. It made her jump up about a foot into the air.

Hay Lin slid over on the bench next to Irma. "Was that thunder, or just your stomach?" she asked.

Now we're in major trouble if Hay Lin is trying to crack jokes! Cornelia thought. That rumble definitely didn't sound like anything in nature . . . or anything normal.

At that moment, Irma's mom stuck her head out the kitchen window. "You'll see," she called out to the girls. "Tomorrow morning you'll have all the sunshine you could want! Dinner will be ready in five minutes!" She sounded a lot more cheerful than any of the girls felt.

Cornelia shivered. But she knew that it wasn't just the chill in the air that was making her cold.

I have to say something, she decided, before I totally freak out. I just can't keep it in anymore.

"I don't like this weather," she said. "It really gives me the creeps." Okay, she thought, that's not all that's on my mind. But at least it's a start.

Taranee nodded, seeming to understood what Cornelia meant. "It's the situation that's scaring us," she said.

Will shrugged. Cornelia thought she seemed a little down. Apparently, she didn't want to say what she was thinking. Which wasn't going to get them anywhere.

"Yeah," Will said. "But for the time being, all we can do is wait." She looked at her friends as she spoke, then went right back to looking at the ground.

Then everyone was silent again. So maybe she's right, Cornelia admitted to herself. But wait for what? Yan Lin said Nerissa was after us. Does she know where we are? How will she get here? What will she do if she finds us? Can we do anything to get ready for her? Are we strong enough to turn her back? And what will happen if we're not?

"Dinnertime!" yelled Irma's brother, breaking Cornelia's train of thought. Christopher's voice was earsplitting, but Cornelia was grateful for the distraction.

Cornelia trooped into the house behind her friends, trying not to worry about the rumbling she had heard in the shrubbery. It was nothing, she told herself. Nothing.

She tried to enjoy Mrs. Lair's dinner, but she couldn't shake the feeling that someone was watching her put each morsel into her mouth— someone who wasn't at the table. After a while she put down her fork. I can't eat, she realized. I'm not even hungry. If I keep this up, I'm going to be sick.

After dinner, Irma suggested that they all play a game. It seemed like a good way to get their minds off their worries. Irma rummaged through a closet and pulled out a fun game called Moneybags, which the girls had played before.

Cornelia selected her playing piece, but her mind wasn't really on the game. It was on Nerissa, then Caleb, then Nerissa again. It took her a moment to bring herself back to reality when it was finally her turn. Cornelia held the dice in her hand and hoped for a seven—it was the only way to avoid the plastic real estate that Irma had bought up and placed all over the game board. As soon as the dice hit the table, though, Irma hooted and pumped her hands in the air.

"Six! Ha!" she gloated. "Bad move! Now you're on my property!"

Is she worried at all about Nerissa? Cornelia wondered. Does anything *ever* get between Irma and having a good time? Sometimes she wished she could be that way, but she wasn't.

"Two motels and a delicatessen," Cornelia said, shaking her head. "You sure have a nose for business, Irma!"

Irma rubbed her hands together gleefully. "Laugh it up all you want, Corny! But start counting your money. This little stop is going to cost you dearly!"

Taranee started to crack up. But even her laughter couldn't conceal the sound that was coming from outside the window. It wasn't the crash of more thunder or the steady drumbeat of the rain on the roof—it was, unmistakably, a person who was making that sound. And the person didn't sound too happy.

Taranee stopped laughing. "What's that?" she asked.

"Somebody screamed!" Cornelia cried. She was suddenly in panic mode.

I knew it! she thought. Something is happening outside! I can just feel it! I knew the sky was not just warning of a storm coming. What if Nerissa herself is outside, waiting for us?

Cornelia ran to the window and pulled up the shade. It was so dark outside that it was hard to see anything. Soon the others—including Irma's mom and brother—were at her side and looking out.

But Irma herself? She was still set on getting rich. "Hey! Hold on!" she whined. "Get back here! I still have to get paid!"

Cornelia looked over her shoulder at Irma. Even though she was a strong Guardian, Irma couldn't help herself and wanted to finish the game. While everyone was gathered at the window, Irma was still counting her money and planning to put up more plastic houses. As Cornelia peered out the window, she wished she knew what evil W.I.T.C.H. was up against now.

NINE

Nerissa squatted at the edge of Mount Thanos, flames shooting into the sky above her, volcanic ash obscuring her vision. She knew now that the fire would yield images to her when the time came. But when would that be? Nerissa felt the weight of every passing second. She could hardly wait for the first phase of her plan to get under way. What is more painful? she wondered. Watching and waiting—or taking a flying leap into this volcano?

Be patient, you have waited all these many centuries, she reminded herself. It will not be long now.

Her memories of the earth were foggy. But Khor *must* have made it to Heatherfield by now, Nerissa figured. And from there it was not far to the shores of Green Bay. That was where the girls had gone to sleep in the woods, soak themselves in water, and cook themselves in the sun. Nerissa sniffed. What a ridiculous way to entertain oneself, she thought. What a waste of precious time. Nerissa was sure that, when she was a Guardian, she had never gone to the beach.

And to think that these girls were now the Guardians! That they, of all people, had been entrusted with treasures they could not comprehend! A memory flashed into Nerissa's mind for a fraction of a second. She and Yan Lin had also been young when they became Guardians. Their strength and energy had served them well.

But look what happened! Nerissa thought angrily. Could a young girl really be trusted with such potent magic? Nerissa quivered with jealousy as she considered the question. She knew the answer in her bones.

What nonsense, she thought. And what fools in Candracar chose these naive youngsters for the job? No mere girl could master the Heart's true power. No! Only I know how to handle it!

Suddenly, a figure appeared in the flames. It was Khor, breaking through a chain-link fence and skulking under a sign that said: CAMP COR-MORAN—PRIVATE PROPERTY.

Private property, Nerissa thought. Nothing is private from me!

With every step Khor took toward the girls, the Heart came closer to Nerissa. She could feel the shape of it on her fingertips, the weight of it in her palm. She could see it sparkle as it summoned the four other great powers of the universe. . . .

Nerissa had tried to give him directions, but Khor could understand only so much. He had the body of a beast, but still the brain of a dog. He stumbled into a clearing surrounded by cabins, and stood right there, where any passerby could spot him.

It's lucky it appears to be raining, thought Nerissa. She had not conjured up the storm on her own, but surely this was further evidence that the elements were with her. Nobody would notice him, she told herself. The weather was too forbidding for anybody to be outside. And the claps of thunder would conceal the noise he made.

Khor sneaked through a grove of trees, water cascading off his armor. Impervious to the wind and rain, he was well positioned to wait out the storm. The darkness would give him cover for his surprise attack.

Nerissa gasped. In the flames now she could see not just one figure, but three. There was Khor . . . and there were two others. Teenagers, by the looks of them. Nerissa snorted with disdain. Nice night for a walk, she thought. Then she observed the figures carefully. If she watched their lips, she was able to understand what they were saying.

"What's wrong, Steve?" asked the girl cheerfully, as if she'd failed to notice the forbidding weather. "I thought we wanted to spend a little time together."

Her boyfriend held the umbrella over her head. "With all of this rain," the boy said, "I'm growing gills, Janine! Why don't we go back to the tent?"

The girl objected. "You're so unromantic," she complained. "I love this weather! The air gets electrified! The pine forest fills with a million aromas!"

Nerissa sniffed. It's just as I thought, she

noted. The young people today are even more ridiculous than they were in my time.

"Please, honey," the boy pleaded. "I've got snails crawling up my nose, and my lungs are growing moss!"

His girlfriend still looked starry-eyed, but she gave in without further argument. "All right, then," she conceded. "But at least let me see another bolt of lightning!"

As if at her command, a bolt of lightning streaked across the sky. It illuminated the drenched trees, the soaked cabins . . . and the figure of Khor, hiding behind the trees and brandishing two hatchets!

Kra-boom!

A thunderclap pierced the air. But it was not enough to obscure the terrified shrieks of the two teenagers, who dashed toward the cabins as if their very lives depended on it. Nerissa smiled as they ran away. There was nothing she enjoyed as much as seeing fear on a person's face.

As if he were after you! she thought. *Why would he ever bother with fools like you?*

The teenagers clung to each other as the doors around them flew open and other campers bombarded them with questions.

"Hey, kids!" a concerned man asked. "What happened?"

The terrified couple could barely get out their story. "Th—there was an armed man in those trees! He was dressed funny, and h—he had an ax or a cleaver or something like that! He . . . he came toward us! And then he stopped . . . and ran off into the woods!"

Another camper was in disbelief. "A man with an ax? But . . ."

The girl burst into tears. "It was so scary! Maybe . . . maybe he's still around here somewhere!"

"We're in danger!" a woman cried. "Somebody, call the sheriff's office! It seems there's an armed man in the area!"

Nerissa shook her head. Such hysteria! she thought. There is no threat to them! These humans take themselves far too seriously.

Then, suddenly, something caught her eye. The door to another cabin had opened, and in it Nerissa could see a group of humans silhouetted in the lamplight.

Is that them? she asked herself.

Nerissa counted them carefully. Seven?

Maybe not. She couldn't be sure.

But five of the figures were girls of just the right age . . .

It was them, Nerissa thought. No doubt about it. There was Yan Lin's offspring—the girl's resemblance was uncanny. There was a girl with long blond braids, and there was one with shorter, brown ones. There was also a woman who seemed to be the mother of the dark-haired girl. And the small boy must be her son. Family members, Nerissa mused. They could come in handy later.

Finally, Nerissa's gaze was drawn to the front of the group. She felt a magnetic force pulling her toward the girl with the unruly mop of red hair and the look of grave concern on her face. Earlier, she had branded this one with her mark, but she had not fully seen the girl until now. The Keeper of the Heart, Nerissa thought, her heart filling with fury—but not for long.

The mother stood nervously at the door, apparently listening to everyone's frantic talk. Turning to the young group behind her and ushering them back inside, she said, "Girls . . . get back in the house, please!"

Had Khor seen them, too? Nerissa

wondered. Was he ready to pounce when the moment was right? It was time to test her line of telepathic communication.

Khor stood on a bluff over the cabins now, watching the campers scurry around in fear. Rain streamed down around him, and yet he did not appear to get wet. Nerissa channeled her voice into a stream of magic that led directly to his brain.

"It was them, Khor!" she exulted. "Did you see them?"

Nerissa could see Khor nodding. So he hears me clearly, she thought. Good.

"Don't attack them tonight!" she ordered. "This place is too crowded. Tomorrow is a new day!" This was her incantation, her reminder that the end of the Guardians was at hand— and, with it, the coming of her new rule.

Khor looked toward the sky and bared his rows of menacing teeth, sharper and more lethal than any dog's.

Nerissa made sure to encourage her warrior. "It is during the wait that a hunter proves himself! And you will know when the right moment has come!"

She could feel a charge in their connection

now, and her final words to him were punctuated by a jagged bolt of lightning and a deafening roar of thunder.

"Go, Khor!" Nerissa howled. "Find a place to spend the night and wait . . . Such is the order of Nerissa!"

She, too, would lie down and wait till daybreak.

TEN

Will folded up her sleeping bag and put a few more things in her backpack before heading out the door.

Beach towel? she asked herself. Check. Sunscreen? Check. And sunglasses. Check.

Mrs. Lair had called it. The storm clouds had blown over during the evening, and this morning the sun was shining. In spite of the previous night's storm, they were going to get a full day at the beach.

One more thing, Will reminded herself, as she looked into her beach bag. Her cell phone! It was all charged up and ready. Now, she lamented, if it would only ring. She was dying to hear from Matt.

As she peered out the window, Will

couldn't believe how bright and sunny the day was turning out to be. Last night had been really spooky. She was still pretty scared about what the couple had said they'd seen in the woods the night before.

Was it a run-of-the-mill ax murderer? Will wondered. Or was it someone coming just for us—like Nerissa? Hay Lin's grandmother did warn us. Not knowing what we are up against is the worst feeling. But I guess we have to wait and see.

That was easier said than done, however. Yan Lin's words kept echoing in Will's mind. *The ancient Guardian will soon return to strike. . . . She wants the Heart of Candracar. . . . She seeks revenge!* Will was feeling more unsettled than she had admitted to her friends. As the leader of W.I.T.C.H., she felt that she had to remain totally strong and focused. But that was not always easy. And this time, she had a sense of just how evil their enemy might be. After all, she'd already encountered Nerissa in her dream. Will wasn't interested in seeing her again anytime soon.

Apparently, Irma thought the couple they had met the previous night had been making up a story. She was still mad about not getting to finish playing the board game. "I think those two were in on it with Cornelia," she laughed as she shut the door to the cabin. "I'm still waiting for my money!"

Nobody said anything. Maybe they were worried, too, Will thought. But Irma seemed oblivious. She continued to chat on and on as they walked to the beach.

"And then, come on," Irma said. "Why would a sane person run around a campground with two chef's knives?"

"A person who wasn't missing a few marbles wouldn't do that. . . ." Hay Lin agreed. "But our friend might just be out of his mind!"

Or maybe we are, Will thought. What if it's Nerissa creeping around out there, and what if we should be planning our getaway instead of hanging out on the beach? Sometimes she wished she could be easygoing, like Irma. But right now she wished Irma could be worried, like her!

The cabin door popped open before the group got very far. Mrs. Lair stood in the doorway, with her hands on her hips. "Are you still talking about what happened last night, girls?

Time to change the subject! The investigation is in capable hands." She looked around at the girls and gave them each a reassuring smile. Then she tossed a small plastic bottle at Irma and added, "See you on the beach—and don't forget the sunscreen!"

She's right, Will thought. We need to lighten up. Or at least I do. We're on vacation! "Sure thing!" she said, waving at Irma's mom as cheerfully as she could. "Your weather forecast was right on, Mrs. Lair!"

Irma's mom smiled, waved, and closed the door. Will managed not to think about the ax murderer for a whole five minutes. She walked behind the cabin, trying to focus on happy things . . . like Matt. She followed the path through the woods to the beach, thinking only of holding Matt's hand. Will we ever go back to the Lodelyday? she wondered idly. Can we have fun in a place a lot less fancy?

And then all at once her problem came flooding back. At the spot just before the path to the beach met the sand stood a man in a uniform, with a crowd of people gathered around him.

"Look! The police!" Taranee said.

The guy's got to be a detective or something, Will thought. Someone is on the case. Better late than never.

She was ready to give him the benefit of the doubt even if there'd been no sign of him the night before.

The man was tall and burly, with a bushy mustache and a uniform that barely fit over his prominent belly. He kept his hand on his holster as he explained gruffly, "I already told you, folks! Everything's under control! My men have been alerted, and they're looking into the situation!"

The crowd didn't exactly seem relieved by the man's announcement. There was still a lot of muttering, and there were still a lot of concerned-looking faces.

"But you haven't even combed the area!" one woman said accusingly to the police officer. "There might still be traces, Detective!"

"After last night's storm," the policeman replied, "the rain will have washed away any clues!"

"Maybe you would have found something if you'd shown up right away last night," someone else grumbled.

The policeman lowered his mirrored sunglasses for a second, then seemed to think better of it and lifted them up again to cover his eyes.

I guess he doesn't want to make eye contact or something, Will thought. He seems to be a little frustrated. But, like they say, if you can't take the heat, get out of the fire. It's part of the guy's job to answer questions from concerned citizens.

"I already told you, there's no danger!" the policeman snapped. "Green Bay is a peaceful place—always has been. And I won't let the late-night hallucinations of two kids get the whole place up in arms!"

His uniform brushed Will's arm as he marched impatiently through the crowd, not even bothering to say, "Excuse me." In his mind, the conversation was over.

"Wait a minute!" Will cried. She had more questions for the officer.

"But, Detective Hamilton!" another man called after him.

It was no use. The policeman put his hand up to stop the questions. "We're at the height of the summer season, folks. A false alarm would just cause panic . . . and that's not going to happen on my watch."

He lumbered over to his car, climbed in, and drove off, with the sirens wailing.

I thought they weren't supposed to flash their lights unless they were on their way to an emergency, Will thought angrily. So much for not making everyone panic.

The other campers scattered off in every direction, muttering to themselves. Will, however, didn't budge.

I don't even want to go to the beach now! she thought stubbornly. We need to get to the bottom of this! This calls for some W.I.T.C.H. action.

"Well, that detective sure has a temper," Taranee said, stating the obvious.

Will smiled. "Seems like Sherlock there thinks Green Bay's reputation is more important than a nut case on the loose!"

"Maybe the detective's right," Hay Lin piped up. "Maybe the couple just imagined it."

Will cringed. This is no time to take things lightly, she thought. This is no time to trust anybody but ourselves. "But maybe they didn't, and that guy just isn't willing to lift a finger to find out!" she shot back. Her frustration was making her a little anxious.

He doesn't want all the families to get upset, she thought. Ignoring public safety in favor of public opinion is never a good idea. But maybe this situation is not a problem this officer can fix. Maybe it's *not* his problem. Maybe it's our very own ax murderer, lying in wait for us. For me. For my four best friends. And for the Heart of Candracar.

At that moment, Will realized that her friends had to take action.

She looked over at Irma. Actually, Will quickly realized, all of her friends were looking to her for what to do next.

"So?" Irma said. "What should we do?"

"So . . ." Will said hesitantly. She adjusted her backpack and stood a little straighter. Feeling more confident, she said, "Count the policeman out."

The girls were a little taken aback at her assessment. As the leader, she had to take charge, and it had become clear that the Guardians were needed here. She knew that, united, they could take on this evil and con- quer it. Hadn't they proven before that they could do battle and win? Now was the time to get a plan in motion.

Will moved over to Cornelia. "I know someone else who could find out what's going on." She gave Cornelia a look. "Right, Corny?"

If this is going to work, Will thought, I need to motivate everyone. We each have a special power, and to solve this mystery, we are all going to have to work together.

ELEVEN

What? Me? Cornelia snapped to attention. What is Will talking about? she wondered. What does she want me to do?

Will was staring at her, as if she expected her to know the answer. As if she wanted her to read her mind.

"Me?" Cornelia said, stalling. "How?" She had no idea what her friend was getting at.

Rolling her eyes, Will gestured to the trees around them. "You have the powers of the earth. The forest is alive. All you have to do is listen to what the trees tell you!"

"Right," Cornelia said. She looked down at the ground wearily.

I guess I can, she thought without much faith in herself. I mean, it's been a while since I used my magic in that way—my regular magic, not the awesome power that I absorbed from the Altermere. But what if I mess it up? What if I let everybody down? That would be just what we need after everything else that's happened.

She realized that everyone was watching her. Will stood waiting, expecting her to come up with an answer. Normally, Cornelia was used to people staring at her, looking to her for the next move. But her confidence was shot. She glanced around her and up at the trees, which were tall and glorious. The earth was her friend. She took one deep gulp of air, and then another. Slowly, she began to relax.

I was chosen to be a Guardian and given these powers for good, she thought. Now I can use my powers over the earth to help. I am strong—even if I don't always feel that way.

Who was this vengeful, hateful force bent on stealing the Heart of Candracar? The story that Hay Lin's grandmother had told them about Nerissa haunted Cornelia. There was no time to lose. She had to do her part.

Without saying anything more to her friends, she walked off a few paces to a patch of grass surrounded by tall pine trees. She listened to the pine needles stirring in the gentle wind, and she took a deep breath of their piney scent. She tried to center herself, to become one with the trees. It wasn't long before all the living things around her were standing at attention, ready to respond. A bunch of dried leaves blew up off the ground and danced around her as if to say hello.

Cornelia wasn't sure how to begin. What's the right question? she wondered. I have to figure out what to ask!

Her mind leaped back to an assignment she'd had in school a long time ago. She had had to pretend to be a reporter doing an interview, and was supposed to ask questions on six subjects: who, what, where, when, why, and how. Her teacher had said that getting answers to these questions would lead her to the center of any story.

I want to know if . . . if . . . She tried to formulate the right question in her mind. I want to know if last night there really was somebody in those trees. Can anyone tell me?

Cornelia focused on her question and mentally transformed it to the eager earth. Was someone there at all? she asked the leaves and grasses, the trees and moss.

Nothing happened.

I want to know if last night there really was somebody in those woods, she repeated. Can anyone answer me? Can you . . . can you hear me? she faltered. She tried to trust her magic, but she wasn't sure she could.

Then, suddenly, a breeze blew around her in her short blue dress. Her eyes were closed, but she could feel the skirt fluttering at her knees. She prepared to receive her answer . . . but instead she felt a bunch of vines shooting out of the ground and wrapping themselves tightly around her ankles!

"Aaagh!" Cornelia yelled.

"Cornelia!" she could hear Taranee screaming.

And then she heard Will, stopping her: "No, wait," Will said. "Don't get near her."

Cornelia had been scared for a moment, but suddenly her fear melted away. Will's right, she thought. This is happening for a reason. The earth is with me, not against me.

The vines were growing more slowly now that they'd stopped her from moving forward.

The green shoots made a low, soft *Wip! Wip!* sound as they emerged from the soil. Cornelia knelt down to stroke them soothingly. She could have sworn the vines were rubbing against her ankles like a bunch of affectionate little kittens.

"Why are you holding me back?" Cornelia asked them. "You don't want me to go further, do you?"

She imagined they were nodding. Or maybe that wasn't her imagination at all. Which meant that what she was looking for was right there, Cornelia told herself.

So talk to me, she demanded, looking at the earth. The vines hugged her so closely that she had to give in to their demands.

Zwwinn!

She became one with the vines as she listened to their story, disappearing with a humming sound and a sudden flash of light.

Images flew through her mind so quickly now that it was like watching a time-lapse film in science class. There was the sun, rising and setting. There were clouds, flying across the sky. There were buds in spring, and green summer leaves, golden autumn leaves, barren stems in snow and ice, then spring again. There were magnificent sunsets and raging storms. Cornelia saw fruit and flowers, birds and insects, growth and decay. It was the tale of the woods, a story without a voice, made of rain and leaves, of cold wind . . .

. . . And silent visitors.

Cornelia had been hypnotized by the story of nature's endless patterns and rhythms. But then she saw some images that were totally out of place. She saw grasses crushed by heavy steps. She saw massive hands twisting the slender trunks of two young bushes. And then she saw an armored monster peering out of a hiding place in the woods. His metal shields and weapons were concealed in the stormy darkness. But one spot glowed brightly in the center of his chest. It was a shape, a crest, that Cornelia had seen before, though she couldn't remember where . . .

She felt the rough terrain of the woods, leading to a dark cave. And she felt the monster's hate. His strength. His determination to track the Guardians down.

"Hey!" she cried. Then, suddenly, the spell was broken. She found herself lying on the ground, her ear to a patch of dirt.

"Hey!" she repeated, springing up and brushing off her dress. She couldn't believe what she had just seen. Was it for real? Had that really happened?

Her friends rushed to her side as Cornelia held her head in her hands. She felt dizzy, unsure of where she was, unsure of what her magic had told her.

"Everything okay, Cornelia?" Will asked, her eyes wide with concern.

Cornelia shook her head from side to side to make sure she was okay. Nothing seemed to be physically wrong with her. Her brain was the problem. She wondered if she would ever be able to erase that awful image from her mind. She closed her eyes for a moment and took a deep breath. I'm fine, she told herself.

"Yeah . . . yeah . . ." Cornelia assured her friends. "I think I'm still in one piece."

Hay Lin cut to the chase. "What happened?" she asked. Did you have some kind of premonition, or what?"

Cornelia reached out and grabbed a tree trunk to steady herself. She didn't want to say what she'd seen—it was so terrible she could hardly bear to describe the scene to her friends—but she had to.

That was the whole point! she told herself sternly. I was supposed to get the information and share it with my friends so we would know what we're facing.

"I'm afraid so," she answered. "Last night there was a really nasty-looking guy creeping around . . ."

Irma interrupted. "Man! We have to talk to the police right away!"

She saw that detective, Cornelia thought angrily. What part of his lazy attitude didn't she understand?

Taranee jumped in. "Okay, Irma," she said sarcastically. "And what do we tell them? That the trees told us?"

Should we tell them that the monster in the woods wasn't human? thought Cornelia. That he was from another world? That he wasn't after vacationing residents, but sent to find the Guardians of the Veil? That would not go over very well.

"No!" she blurted out. "The police won't be able to do anything! That creature was here for us."

She took a deep breath before she offered up the most troubling of the things she'd seen. She now knew where she had seen the crest that was on the creature's chest. This mystery was getting pretty easy to figure out.

"He had a symbol on his chest," she began. "Nerissa's symbol . . ."

TWELVE

Bree-Bree! Breeep!

Will's cell phone rang for what had to be the millionth time that day.

Not that I'm counting or anything, Irma fumed. *Not that it's bothering me in any way,* she thought as she gritted her teeth.

After Cornelia's chat with the trees, the girls had headed for the beach. There they were going to try to keep occupied and enjoy the day. They knew that the creature wouldn't bother them at the beach in the daytime. But no one was really having any fun—they were all pretending, just going through the motions. This was not the vacation that Irma had planned on. She had thought that she and her friends would have been laughing and joking around by then, meeting cute boys and having a summer splash.

Bree-Bree! Breeep!

Will took her phone from the side pocket of her backpack. Her smile was wide, and her face bright pink.

Irma, though, was seeing red.

Was it because she was sitting in a line of beach chairs with her friends, watching the brilliant sunset over Cormoran Beach? Was it because she was basking in the glow of a happy day? It most certainly was not.

Actually, the more Irma thought about the present situation, the madder she got. The whole thing was ridiculous.

I've been stewing all day, she thought. And now I'm just about ready to boil over!

Hugging her knees to her chest, she wrapped her pink towel around herself and counted up the reasons she was feeling so totally furious.

Okay. So, first, we've spent the whole day chatting about Nerissa's henchman or whatever he is, she thought. We talked and talked. We looked at the problem from every angle, but there's still really no plan. We don't know what to do, because we have to rely on a bunch of trees for our information! How can we fight someone who we don't know exists?

So what did we accomplish today? Not a thing! raged Irma. Our big plan is to wait around and see what happens. Nobody wants to talk to the police. Nobody wants to do anything, exactly. We're just waiting. Just existing here at Camp Cormoran, when we could be having fun.

This is a vacation, people, Irma wanted to yell at her friends. *Remember? When do we flirt with the lifeguards? And when do we paint our toenails and do our hair? When did everybody forget how to have a good time? That's what friends are supposed to do! Not mope around and worry.*

Irma looked at her arms.

White as snow, she thought. So much for my tan. At this point I'd be having more fun if my friends hadn't even come, for crying out loud. At this point, I wouldn't mind hanging out with my little brother! At least Christopher likes to get a little sun and to swim at the beach. At least he's not a total stress case.

And the worst thing of all? About every two

seconds, Will's phone was ringing, with a text message from Matt. Will seemed to go all weak in the knees when Matt sent a message. Weak in the head, too. Just what they needed in their leader right now.

It's understandable—I'll grant her that, Irma thought. She's in love. Or in *like*, anyway. But why is everyone else so worked up about it? You'd think nobody here had ever had a boyfriend before! Boys come and go, thought Irma, wisely. But what matters is the five of us girls and this chance we have to be together.

Breep!

The phone rang *again*, and Will checked the screen, as if her life depended on it.

"Is it him?" Hay Lin asked breathlessly, as if she'd been waiting all day.

Will nodded, reading Matt's message and talking to Hay Lin at the same time. "Yep, it's Matt!" she announced, as if it were breaking news. "He's on the beach, and he says hi!"

"Again?" Cornelia asked.

At least *someone* sees how ridiculous this is, Irma thought. She gave Cornelia a silent "Thank you" look.

Cornelia's face broke out in a smile. She

wasn't with Irma at all. She was excited for Will. "You guys have been saying hi all day!" Cornelia said. "That must be the eighth message like that." She spoke as if she were some kind of relationship expert.

Hay Lin laughed. "Only the eighth?" she joked. "I counted twelve!"

Taranee wrapped her arm around Will. "I think it's something serious!" she said, making the diagnosis they'd all been waiting for.

Will sent a quick message back to Matt, covering it so no one could see. She brushed off what Taranee had said. "Oh, you're just saying that because you're jealous!"

Suddenly Irma had a sinking feeling. It'll be nothing but Matt, Matt, Matt for the rest of the week, she thought. And when we're not talking about Matt we'll be talking about Nerissa. I can forget about having any fun! I think I need a vacation from this vacation.

It was enough to make her explode, once and for all.

She turned to Will, scowling. "Why don't you turn off that cell phone?" she barked. "Can't you see we have more important things to think about?"

Will looked at her like a wounded puppy, which made Irma even angrier. She jumped up and pointed dramatically toward the woods at the edge of the beach. "Don't forget that out there there's a creep ready to chop us to pieces!"

Cornelia grimaced. "And to think that this morning you were the least worried of us all!" she said. As usual, her cool manner made Irma even angrier.

Will jumped up and looked Irma in the eye. "We're not underestimating the danger, Irma!" she said, in a tone that was probably supposed to sound concerned, but was actually a bit stern. "But luckily nothing serious has happened yet."

"But something *could* happen at any moment, Will," Irma said, through clenched teeth. She bit her tongue and kept the rest of her thoughts to herself. She was afraid of what she'd say if she really let it fly.

Could she talk down to me a little more? Irma wondered. Make sure I really understand? Guess what? I *do* get what's going on here! Our vacation has been ruined! Thanks to old Nerissa and her sidekick. Thanks to Will and

Matt. Thanks to my bunch of so-called friends . . .

Then Taranee spoke up. "I still don't get who you're mad at. . . ."

Irma was about to go ballistic. Who am I mad at? she thought wildly. Oh, I'll tell you! You guys, for coming here. Yan Lin, for telling us something we'd rather not know. That wacko guy in the woods, for sneaking around where he's not wanted.

Irma was ready to blurt it all out . . . when suddenly, she had another thought.

I'm mad that we can't stop talking about Nerissa, Irma thought. But I'm mad when Matt's the topic, too. I'm mad that we don't have a plan—but I don't want to have a plan, either. I just want to relax. It doesn't make any sense!

"I'm not mad at anybody!" Irma cried. "And that's what makes me even angrier!" Suddenly she could see that it was a little funny.

Irma took a deep breath as her temper cooled. Then she admitted to herself and the others what was really on her mind. "This was supposed to be our first vacation together! And here we are, standing around on the beach, waiting for the next monster up at bat! It's not a vacation at all—it's just more of what we always do!"

It's not fair! she thought. It's not right!

Will gave her a funny half-smile and tucked some of her hair behind an ear. "Nobody ever said that being the Guardians of the Veil was going to be easy," she said.

Irma sighed. "I know," she said. "It's just that this is an enormous responsibility. . . . I realize that more and more every day."

I just want to have a normal trip to the beach! she thought. Is that so much to ask?

But even Irma knew the answer to that one. There might *never* be another normal trip to the beach, she reminded herself. That's part of the job. We're Guardians. That is just the way it is.

She sighed. It's not that I don't love being a Guardian, she thought, but why can't we get a breather once in a while? I loved being normal, too! And what's happening on this vacation is definitely *not* normal!

But, she thought, I guess that we weren't chosen because we were normal girls. We were each chosen because we have strength and power. We're better than normal! Yes, we are the chosen Guardians, and we have to defend ourselves.

Now Irma felt able to channel her anger. She was focused and sure.

Watch out, Nerissa! She thought. You don't know who you are battling. You haven't encountered W.I.T.C.H.!

THIRTEEN

Hay Lin impulsively threw her arms around Irma. Poor Irma! she thought. She knew that Irma had planned this trip and wanted everyone to have a good time. Forever the optimist, Hay Lin felt sure the vacation would improve, if only Irma could be patient. She gave Irma one of her trademark smiles. "Today is a new day!" she said.

"I think so, too," Irma agreed.

But something else seemed to be on Irma's mind. Hay Lin took a step back to give her friend a little space and a chance to speak.

"I don't want my mom and my brother to get stuck in the middle of all this," Irma said, clenching her fists. "We've got to defend ourselves."

Then Taranee snapped into action. "I know! Tonight we'll sleep in shifts. We'll take turns standing guard!"

Though Hay Lin knew that they had to face a difficult battle, she wasn't in the mood to talk about strategies just then. She felt odd, and sort of exhausted. She'd wanted to make Irma feel better, but she didn't feel so great herself.

It's probably from all the worrying we've done today, she thought. What I really need is a good nap.

Taranee's suggestion gave Hay Lin the opening that she was looking for. "Well, if you guys don't mind," she said, "I'll start right now!"

"Start what? Standing guard?" Irma asked, skeptical again. "In broad daylight?"

Hay Lin giggled. "No, sleeping!' she replied.

She grinned at her friends until they grinned back. Then she made her preparations. Cornelia's towel would do for a bed—she wasn't using it at the moment, after all. And Cornelia's bag would make a perfect pillow! Hay Lin was glad she'd worn the T-shirt that matched her towel. Both had kooky green alien faces on them.

It's never a bad time for coordinated accessories, Hay Lin thought. Even when you're asleep!

She curled up and closed her eyes contentedly, soaking in the last bit of warm evening sun. From a few feet away, she could hear her friends' voices.

"Getting right down to business, isn't she?" sniffed Cornelia.

"Sleep well, Hay Lin. And sweet dreams," said Taranee.

It won't be for long, Hay Lin promised herself. I just need a little pick-me-up to recharge my batteries!

Finally she felt relaxed, and she closed her eyes. Her thoughts turned to her visit with her grandmother. It hadn't been the kind of visit she'd expected. And, with all the craziness, she hadn't really had a chance to think about what her grandmother had told them.

Grandma did look very worried, Hay Lin thought. And had she imagined it, or had her grandmother's good-bye hug felt a little tighter and longer than usual? What did she know that the Guardians didn't know? Hay Lin wondered.

Grandma said she couldn't predict how

Nerissa will strike, or when, thought Hay Lin. But why didn't she tell us more about Nerissa herself? What was she leaving out? And why? Maybe it's painful for her to talk about. But it could be painful for us not to know!

Hay Lin's mind raced until it came to a sudden stop, as unseen forces dragged her into sleep. In a matter of seconds, she was drifting away from all the cares of the day and floating into a dream.

In the dream, it was already dark on the beach. Swimmers and sunbathers had gone inside for the evening, and the only sound was the constant crashing of the waves. A thick layer of clouds obscured the stars and moon, but an eerie light still danced on the water.

Hay Lin dreamed that she woke up on this nighttime beach. She looked around for her friends, but they were gone. She searched for something familiar, but suddenly Cormoran Beach seemed as far away and foreign as the moon.

And then she heard a voice.

I see you, Hay Lin, it hissed. *Even when you hide. Yes, even when you close your eyes.*

In her dream, Hay Lin sat up on her towel.

She looked in the direction where she thought the cabins were—but she realized that no voice could carry from so far away.

"Who are you?" she asked the voice nervously. "What do you want from me?" Her stomach muscles clenched in fear.

There was no answer.

Even in her heavy slumber, Hay Lin dimly remembered the reports of the armed man in the woods.

What if it's him? she thought. I have to get back to my friends, wherever they are! I'm going to need some help!

She stood up and turned around to gather her belongings. . . .

. . . And what she saw was much worse than any armed man.

A pair of liquid eyes glared at her from the shore. At first she was confused, until the eyes started coming closer. Then it became clear that the eyes belonged to a creature.

That creature crept toward her through the mist until she could see the figure clearly. It was an enormous snake, coiling out of the water toward her, its eyes and fangs shining in the thin light. It loomed over Hay Lin now, just inches from her. Its long tongue lashed out.

"I see you!" the snake whispered. "The two of us are inseparable, Hay Lin, because you are a part of me!"

Hay Lin yanked her towel away, shrieking "N—no! This . . . this is just a dream!"

The snake chuckled ominously. "This is no dream," it said. "This is your worst nightmare, little one, and soon it will be painfully real!"

Before Hay Lin could move another muscle, the snake lunged for her, screaming more than hissing. It tossed her into the air as easily as it might have thrown a beach ball. Then, once she was airborne, the snake began to wind its body around her, beginning with her belly and working its way steadily toward her neck. The snake squeezed so hard that Hay Lin was nearly breathless. And with every passing second, its grip grew tighter, its reach longer. . . .

"Wh-why are you doing this to me?" Hay Lin gasped, while she still could. "Let me go! Let me go! Let me go!" she pleaded.

"You will be the first, Hay Lin," the snake hissed. "And after you, it will be your friends' turn to end up in the clutches of Nerissa!"

Hay Lin's heart went haywire. It was beating

so quickly she was sure it would leap out of her chest. But Grandma . . . Hay Lin thought in her dream . . . and my friends!

"Help!" she bellowed into the silent night.

And then the snake slithered into the ocean, its tail still gripping Hay Lin, ready to submerge her in the cold, dark water. . . .

"Help!" Hay Lin screamed again.

This time, her eyes popped open to see not only the lingering traces of a sunset, but the familiar faces of her friends.

Irma was the first to notice Hay Lin's wide-open eyes. She pointed and joked, "Sleeping Beauty is back among us!"

"Slept badly, huh?" Taranee asked.

Hay Lin collapsed back onto the sand, trying to get hold of herself. She wasn't exactly well rested after her nap.

Was it a dream? The snake was so real! she asked herself. Not like a dream at all, but like a vision of the future. And I don't think that snake was just a snake. I think it was . . . it had to be . . . Nerissa!

In a quavering voice, Hay Lin tried to explain her nightmare. But she couldn't begin to describe the size of the snake or the utter horror it provoked. She only managed to say, "It . . . it was terrible! Nerissa . . . She . . . spoke to me!"

Taranee rushed to her side. "Her again!" she said. "She's back?"

Will knelt down on the blanket next to Hay Lin. "She got into your dreams, too?" she asked.

She knows what it's like, Hay Lin thought as she gave Will a grateful look. Hay Lin knew that Will could relate. After that visit from Nerissa she felt cold, as if she would never be warm again.

Will set her jaw. "I don't like any of this one bit!" she said. "We have no way to defend ourselves against invasions like this!"

It's true, Hay Lin thought. I'll never feel safe sleeping knowing that Nerissa can sneak into my mind like that.

Hay Lin felt almost paralyzed. She's going to get us one by one, she thought. Who knows what she'll do next? I think that that dream was not even the worst of what Nerissa is capable of doing.

Her teeth were chattering so badly that Hay Lin could hardly get her words out. But she knew that she had to relate the dream to her friends. Any information that they had would be helpful.

"She's about to attack us!" Hay Lin stuttered. "And she said that . . . that . . . I'll be her first target!"

FOURTEEN

Cornelia remained silent.

I mean, really, what can I say? she wondered. Poor Hay Lin looks like she's seen a ghost—her face is almost as green as that alien on her shirt! And I bet Taranee and Irma are thinking the same thing I'm thinking: when is Nerissa going to come for *us*? She's already gotten to Will and Hay Lin. It's only a matter of time before she infiltrates our dreams, too.

Will bustled around, folding beach chairs and tossing water bottles into beach bags. "Let's go; it's getting chilly," she said, as if the weather were their biggest problem. She didn't say anything about Nerissa or Hay Lin.

Cornelia didn't know or care where her pink sweater was just then. She had a feeling she'd be freezing whether she had it on or not.

They set off single file for the cabin: Will in front, with Hay Lin following her, Cornelia close on Hay Lin's heels, and Irma and Taranee bringing up the rear.

Cornelia was lost in thought, not watching where she was going—but suddenly she heard a *fwoosh!* and saw Hay Lin disappear before her very eyes!

"Ah!" Hay Lin screamed.

Will and Irma turned and rushed to Hay Lin's side. Hay Lin was sinking into what seemed like quicksand.

"What is going on?" demanded Irma, as if she were looking for someone to blame.

"Help!" Hay Lin screamed. The hole in the sand had opened up further and seemed as if it were ready to swallow her whole.

We have to do something fast! Cornelia thought.

Will dived toward the sand. She scrambled flat on her belly to the edge of the hole. Cornelia rushed to grab hold of Will's ankles while Will waved her arm inside the hole and grabbed Hay Lin's hands.

"Don't be afraid, Hay Lin!" she cried. "I've

got you! Don't worry! I'm here."

Hay Lin's mouth opened and closed as if she were trying to say something. Then, in a weird voice, she said, "But today is a new day!" Cornelia wasn't sure whom she sounded like, but she definitely didn't sound like Hay Lin.

With Irma and Taranee anchoring her, Will managed to grab Hay Lin. Now it was just a matter of hauling her back onto a solid patch of sand. Hay Lin wasn't heavy, but she'd already sunk way down. Cornelia pulled Will with all her might, Will pulled Hay Lin, and somehow Hay Lin managed to hold on.

"Aaagh!" Hay Lin screamed.

Cornelia started to worry. What if they couldn't pull Hay Lin up? At that thought, she gave an extra-hard tug.

Slowly but surely, they were pulling Hay Lin closer and closer!

"Irma," Taranee said, "I swear, this is the last time I'm going on vacation with you!"

Irma was happy to see Hay Lin in one piece and gave her a playful smile. But Cornelia could tell that the whole thing had really freaked Irma out. It's not her fault, Cornelia thought. But I bet she feels responsible because this is all happening at her house.

"What's going on with this beach?" Irma said. "Nothing like this has ever happened before!"

Hay Lin confirmed her worst suspicions. "Get me out of here!" she begged tearfully. "There's something down there, and it touched my foot!"

With one final tug, Will freed Hay Lin from the hole.

Cornelia took a look at her friend and sighed. "Oh, boy," she said.

Hay Lin looked paler than she had before.

Will jumped into the hole. "Cover me, Cornelia!" she cried.

There was no time to argue. Cornelia leaped in after her. They landed at the bottom of the gigantic sand pit.

A flash of blue caught Cornelia's eye. It was something in the wall of the sand pit, buried well beneath the surface of the sand: an opening.

"Oh!" said Will, her eyes following Cornelia's.

That's strange, Cornelia thought. "What's in there?" she asked. With her hand, she brushed the sand away from the hole. It's like a port-hole, she thought. Or a tunnel. So this was under us the whole time we were on the beach? Who was waiting here? Who was listening to us? She wasn't sure she wanted to know the answers, but she was determined to find them anyway.

When she'd uncovered it entirely, Cornelia saw that the opening was taller than she was. It led into a long passageway that seemed to head toward the water. Cornelia couldn't see the end of it. She couldn't figure out what it was made of, either. The material was translucent and glistening, with a blue sheen. Was it ice? she wondered. But it couldn't be ice. Then something clicked in her mind, and she remembered a fact from who knew where. This stuff had to be glass!

She reached into the tunnel to touch the wall and see if her hunch was correct. She drew her hand back quickly. Yup, she thought.

"These walls are scorching hot," she told Will. "Some incredible source of heat must have turned the sand into glass!"

Will shook her head. "Couldn't have been anything natural," she pointed out. "It's like the rest of the weird stuff that's been going on."

"Do you think Nerissa did this?" Cornelia asked as she took a couple of steps into the passageway.

"This is just one of her warnings," Will guessed. "She's closing in on us, and then . . . who knows?"

Suddenly Cornelia heard a thud behind her. This is it, she thought. Nerissa has us cornered.

It wasn't Nerissa at all, though. It was a floppy-haired guy in a flowered shirt, who seemed to have decided he had to rescue them.

"Girls, what were you thinking?" he said, sounding annoyed. "You need to get out of here right now!"

"Huh? Oh, sure," Cornelia mumbled.

"Um . . . okay," Will said.

The girls looked at each other, but there was nothing they could do. We'll just have to come back later, Cornelia vowed to herself. Did he see what we saw?

The guy in the flowered shirt helped both her and Will out of the sand pit. "You're crazy, girls!" he said. "Another cave-in could have buried you alive!"

"Well, we were just . . . um . . . kidding

around," Will stammered lamely.

Cornelia's mind was full of questions. What was at the end of that tunnel? If they knew where Nerissa was hiding, she thought, maybe they'd have a chance of stopping her. Cornelia could hardly wait to talk it over with her friends.

But as soon as she emerged from the pit, Cornelia saw that the quiet beach had become crowded again. A police car had appeared out of nowhere, and people were milling around it, hoping for information. Probably the detective's cruiser was hiding nearby, Cornelia speculated, just waiting for something to happen.

She had no idea what the police were saying to the people who had gathered, but she could tell that some of the beach residents were panicking. Someone ran by her shouting, "Let's clear out of here, quick!" as if the whole beach were about to go under.

Then she heard a policeman holler into his walkie-talkie. "Get all these folks out of the area, Bob! I'll radio Detective Hamilton!"

No wonder people are scared! Cornelia thought. They're being herded away, but nobody's telling them anything.

"I'm really curious to hear how the detective explains this one!" Will muttered.

Cornelia was curious, too, but not so much about what the police would say. The police investigation was one thing, but the investigation that really mattered would be the one the Guardians did.

We can put together a search party as soon as they're gone, Cornelia thought. We have to explore that passage, whatever it takes.

Nerissa was out there . . . waiting.

FIFTEEN

This has got to be the longest meal of my life, thought Will, looking down at the heaping plate of spaghetti and meatballs that Irma's mom had handed her.

Will had her mind on the beach. She couldn't help thinking about what had happened to Hay Lin. Nerissa was getting closer. Will could feel it.

Irma had already told her mother that the girls would be heading back to the beach right after dinner. Of course, her mother probably thought the girls were going to hang out and build a bonfire or engage in some other fun activity. Maybe some of the kids at the beach would be doing that, but not the five Guardians. Not tonight, anyway.

Will knew they'd be taking a big risk going back into that sandy tunnel, but it was the only way she could think of to change their fates. Nerissa was intent on finding them.

But what if we find her first? Will wondered. It would be good to take her by surprise, Will figured, but she wasn't sure what they would do then.

Irma's little brother was telling a joke, his mouth full of spaghetti. Will decided that she could tune him out as long as she laughed when everyone else did. She had a lot on her mind—Nerissa and Matt.

First, she thought, I have to worry about matters of life and death. Then, maybe—just maybe—I can get down to this love stuff. There's no question about what comes first. I have a great responsibility. And my friends need me. I hate to admit it, but Matt just has to wait.

Will's seat was facing the window, so she was the first one to notice the swirling lights of the police car outside. She jumped to the window just in time to see Detective Hamilton close his car door and strut arrogantly toward the cabins.

Soon the cabin doors popped open one by one, and their occupants streamed outside. Will looked at Irma and raised an eyebrow. Irma nodded, signaling that she thought it was okay to go outside even though they were in the middle of dinner. And when Will opened the door, all of her friends came with her. Even Mrs. Lair and Christopher came along!

Guess I'm not the only one who wants to know what this guy has to say, Will thought. It was good to know she wasn't alone.

In the clearing outside, Detective Hamilton raised his hand to quiet the growing crowd. He bared his teeth in a foolish grin.

The girls pushed forward to get a closer view.

"Nothing's happened, folks!" the detective said, in a voice that was slightly too loud. As the crowd quieted down, he continued. "It was a simple, run-of-the-mill, spontaneous cave-in, caused by marine erosion." He didn't look any-one in the eye as he spoke.

"What's he's saying is crazy," Cornelia whis-pered to Will.

"Even worse, Cornelia!" Will said. "He's lying, and he knows it!"

I hate when grown-ups don't tell the truth, Will thought. I mean, okay, maybe nobody would believe the truth if they heard it—a glass tunnel under a beach *is* pretty strange. But why pretend that everything's under control when it's not? How does that help a bunch of not-so-happy campers?

It just reminded Will that they couldn't rely on anyone to conduct their search for them. This was a case where the police couldn't help. The police had no idea what they were dealing with.

The detective's voice droned on. "For a few more days, a section of beach will be closed off, but I've inspected the area with experts, and I can assure you that everything will soon be back to normal."

He looked around and waited about a fraction of a second for questions. With none coming, he breathed an audible sigh of relief and made a sad attempt to joke about the situation. "You people from Cormoran sure are keeping me busy. I hope I don't see your pretty faces again until at least next season."

People started heading back to their cabins, and the detective hastened back to his car.

Will and her friends followed the crowd back toward the cabins. But then Will noticed that the window of the police car was slightly open.

Maybe I can hear what they are saying, she thought.

Soon she heard a voice from the driver's side say, "Problems, Detective?"

"More than I deserve, Jeremy!" Detective Hamilton grumbled. Then his voice dropped. "What happened underneath that beach is the strangest darned thing I've ever seen," he whispered. "I hate to do it . . . but I'm afraid I'll have to call in for help on this case!"

Will smiled. Just as I thought, she gloated. They're stumped! This isn't a job for the police. It's a job for the Guardians!

She was practically quivering with anticipation as she returned to her friends.

We'll check out that tunnel, she told herself. And we will face whoever is lurking there. I know we can take them on—together. We are the Power of Five.

Will's internal monologue continued: This will be our first dangerous mission since Cornelia came back. And we're ready! After all we've been through, we can handle Nerissa.

Bree-bree! Breep!

Will's hand flew to the pocket of her jeans.

"Let me guess?" said Taranee. "It's Matt, right?"

Will beamed. "Just saying good night to me! Isn't that sweet?" She sent her own good-night message to Matt. Irma couldn't keep from teasing her.

"Good night?" Irma said. "It isn't even ten yet. The night is young!"

"In half an hour, it will be late!" Mrs. Lair warned. "Time flies when you're on vacation. I expect you back in the cabin at curfew, okay?"

Will hung up with Matt and wondered: curfew? That word hadn't come up since they'd been at Camp Cormoran.

"In half an hour?" Irma asked.

"And not a minute later," Mrs. Lair said firmly. "You have time for another walk . . . but stay away from the beach."

This isn't good, Will thought. We can't let her stop us!

It had been a long time since Will had tried to use her telepathic connection with her friends. This was as good a time as any to try it out again. Using her magic, she spoke directly to her friends' minds.

The beach? But that's exactly where I was thinking of going! I want to take another look at the underground passage.

Hay Lin looked skeptical. *But there are two cops guarding it!*

We could get around them—there's a sort of underwater tunnel, Cornelia suggested silently.

That's more like it, Will thought. The old can-do spirit!

Irma was still sulking about her mom's rules. *If you guys really feel up to it.*

Will snapped into leadership mode. She led the way from the cabin, since there wasn't a moment to lose. "Of course we do," she said in her regular voice as soon as they were out of earshot of Mrs. Lair. "We might find out something about Nerissa!"

Hay Lin nodded, so Will would know that she agreed. And Taranee put her arm around Hay Lin in a show of support.

After that, even Irma came around. "Okay. So we'll get to the beach by crossing over the highway!" She motioned in that direction and added, "But let's hurry!"

The girls slinked out of Camp Cormoran and back to the main road. When there was a break in the traffic, they climbed one by one over a rail and slid down a steep hill. They landed on the other side of the beach, behind the officers who were guarding the sand pit. The men stood staring at the cabins, as if they expected trouble to come from that direction.

Catching her breath, Will looked out at the water. Hay Lin came up beside her.

"So far, so good," she said. "Now what?"

Will wasn't sure. She had no plan, and she had no idea what they were facing.

But I have backup, she thought: the four best friends I could hope for—and the four strongest, too! So let's take this one step at a time. Start at the beginning. When we all work together, Nerissa will not stand a chance. She can try to haunt us in our dreams, but we will fight her and win. The Heart is ours . . . and we will prevail.

Will could looked at the sand pit. The police would be a problem, but something else was bothering her. Up in the sky the moon was full, casting a bright white light down on the nighttime beach. It was as if a huge spotlight were being shone down on the sand.

"We have to avoid being seen!" Will whispered to her friends. "With the moon so full, it's as if it were high noon!"

How could they get around without being seen? Will wondered. Quickly, she begin to devise a plan. The plan had to work. Their lives depended on it. And so did the Heart.